Growing up about an hour north of Toronto, Nick Sutcliffe led the life of the typical high school loser. This in turn led him to delve into reading and writing fantasy as a means to escape the mundane boredom of daily life. Going to school for drama in Windsor, Nick found solider footing as he forged his path as an entertainer, writer and the self-proclaimed king of procrastinators.

For S, D, & R: Your impact on my life cannot be put into words. I hope my impact on you is a fraction of what you've done for me.

Nick Sutcliffe

Supernaturalis Mortem

Austin Macauley Publishers™
London • Cambridge • New York • Sharjah

This is a work of fiction. Names, characters, businesses, places, events, locales, and incidents are either the products of the author's imagination or used in a fictitious manner. Any resemblance to actual persons, living or dead, or actual events is purely coincidental.

Ordering Information
Quantity sales: Special discounts are available on quantity purchases by corporations, associations, and others. For details, contact the publisher at the address below.

Publisher's Cataloging-in-Publication data
Sutcliffe, Nick
Supernaturalis Mortem

ISBN 9781685629434 (Paperback)
ISBN 9781685629441 (Hardback)
ISBN 9781685629465 (ePub e-book)
ISBN 9781685629458 (Audiobook)

Library of Congress Control Number: 2023906369

www.austinmacauley.com/us

First Published 2023
Austin Macauley Publishers LLC
40 Wall Street 33rd Floor, Suite 3302
New York, NY 10005
USA

mail-usa@austinmacauley.com
+1 (646) 5125767

Chapter 1
The Dutiful Servant

My sickness had finally caught up with me. As I crawl to the shrine of my goddess at the junction of the three roads, my lifeblood flowed out through my fingers and onto the gravel. The great goddess, my goddess, Hecate had kept her promise; she'd kept me safe in the shadows all these years. And for that, I'd eternally be in her debt, should she ever need my services in the next life.

For sixteen years, Hecate had protected me and my killings. For sixteen years I wandered the world and killed indiscriminately. And for sixteen years, all Hecate had required of me for her protection was that whenever I come across anything dealing with the worship of her, I stop and offer a sacrifice of flesh, blood and bone. I think that the body of my final victim and myself, at the same altar that our covenant was first forged, would be proof enough that I had not ever faltered in my worship.

As I raised my bloody hand to the statuette of Hecate in the shrine, my dying eyes played the same trick on me they did all those years ago. For once my hand touched the image of my goddess, I could have sworn it looked upon me with a look both pleased and saddened. "O, goddess of the hidden," I said. "My soul is yours, a-a-a-a final pay…ment for your protection."

My strength had finally fled my dying body, as I fell to the ground. My last words, nigh, my last breath, a praise to Hecate, my great goddess.

Chapter 2
Medea

Medea looked up to the sky, seeing the crescent moon veiled by a wall of clouds. She seemed to be seeing a shrouded moon more and more of late, especially since her grandmother had first suggested the idea of summoning the demon, and she wasn't sure if it was a good or bad omen. But she knew how she felt about her grandmother's plan, and it wasn't the ceaseless fervor that her mother gave it. But then again, her mother Circe had always been all in on everything her grandmother had said. While it was true that ever since the empire had converted to Christianity, her and her family's worship of the old gods and practice of magic had become the grounds for much prejudice towards her family, Medea still felt that these people didn't deserve to die.

But Medea had never had the words or power to change the minds of her mother and grandmother.

Dressed as she was, in a black translucent slip identical to the ones worn by her mother and grandmother, any passerby would be able to see her perky breasts should the moon ever come out from behind the clouds. A slight breeze brought a slight chill to her body that made her nipples harden, but Medea ignored the unusual cold of the fall night. It was almost time to begin the summoning ritual.

Pulling herself out of her musings, Medea began to gather her magics; a process that her mother and grandmother have promised will come easier when she is more dedicated to her craft for as long as she could remember. Medea had begun to suspect that there was a ritual involved, but she never heard either Hecate or Circe discuss it. But as she was still lacking in this area of magic, her mother and grandmother had sent her ahead of them to ensure that she would be ready when the time came. Kneeling hunched over as if in supplication, she closed her eyes and took a deep breath. With her hands, Medea felt the earth around her, willing Terra's power to strengthen her own. Releasing the breath, she opened her eyes and felt Mother Earth's energy increase her own as she stood once again.

Her senses of sight and hearing now empowered, Medea looked ahead to where the road she stood in the middle of met two others at a shrine to the goddess Trivia that had been there since the time before Alexander the Great. Her ears perked up at the sound of thunder rolling, announcing the arrival of her mother and grandmother; the summoning was about to start.

At the sound of her grandmother's horn (supposedly made from the horn of Asterion himself), Medea began the slow trek toward the junction of the three roads and the shrine of Trivia. Even in the near blackness that the shrouded moon did little to help dissolve, Medea could clearly see the figures of her mother and grandmother as the three of them converged at the shrine. Pulling back the hood of her slip, Medea's grandmother took in the sight of her daughter and granddaughter.

In her earliest memories, Medea could barely remember her grandmother looking like an older version of her daughter, but now she was only the scary, gnarled old woman that children warned each other of in the street, daring each other to get closer to show their foolish bravery. Hecate looked every bit the crone that she represented in their family's coven. Her skin was marred by the lines of age and appeared to be as dry as the remains of mummified pharaohs. Her lower jaw stuck out almost unnaturally and revealed that she only had four teeth left in her entire mouth. But by far the most unsettling feature of her grandmother's visage was her eyes: her right eye was milky white from cataracts, while her left appeared to be sewn shut. But despite this, her vision was preternaturally sharp, as she was able to see things like a hawk sees a mouse in a field.

"Tonight," her grandmother said in her raspy voice. "Tonight, we begin the process of returning the Empire to the old ways. What we start tonight, shall not be concluded until the false god is wiped from history and the real gods are being honored once again. And magic will once again rule the night!

"For too long, have we been persecuted for practicing the old ways. For too long has our faith been ridiculed for being wrong and backward When Caesar built this empire, he brought its conquered territories' gods back to Rome with him. At least back then you could worship any god you saw fit to deign with your praise. But when Theodosius declared Christianity the official religion of the empire, he made us and others like us outsiders to Rome. Well, if we're to be outsiders to Rome, then I suppose that attacking her citizens to protest our case is a declaration of war. And make no mistake, daughter and granddaughter, for we are at war. Our very way of life is under attack, and I'd rather spend eternity in the pits of Tartarus than be forced to change to appease the mindless masses."

"I wholeheartedly agree, mother," Circe voiced her agreement to the words spoken. "I—"

"Do not interrupt me when I'm talking, Circe!" Hecate chastised. "It's nearly midnight; the time has come." From the folds of her slip, Medea's mother produced a small but wide cauldron that rested on a three-legged stand. Placing it between the three of them so that each leg was pointed to a member of the coven, Circe straightened as her mother continued. "Now, for this spell to work, we must all circle the cauldron three times in unison, while saying the words seven times each. "I'll start, then you Circe and then Medea." Looking directly at Medea, her grandmother asked her in a tone that clearly indicated that the answer better be positive, "Did you bring the snakeskin and pine needles?"

Rather than answer verbally, Medea produced the snakeskin and pine needles from a fold in her slip. Wrapping the former around the latter, Medea dropped the ingredients into the cauldron, and with a snap of her fingers, ignited them on fire. But this was no ordinary flame, this was nightfire: the flames of the underworld itself. The flames were blacker than black and seemed to draw what little light there was into themselves.

Her grandmother's next words were spoken in Hebrew, and were words Hecate and Circe had spent the past fortnight perfecting to ensure the right results. "*I call upon*

Trivia and Nemesis to aid in my endeavor. I summon a servant of Trivia to bring about my just revenge; one unafraid and able to perform acts worthy of the just Nemesis and in the name of the great Trivia. Arise, Witchcraft's Vengeance!" As soon as her grandmother had started talking, all three women had begun to circle the cauldron; stepping in unison, with their right hands raised, creating a barrier that bounced and magnified their magics off each other's. And as each woman finished speaking the spell, the next in line would repeat it, louder and faster than the woman before her.

As Medea said the incantation, the irony was not lost on her that they were using Hebrew to summon a demon to kill those that practiced the faith of the Hebrews; but she did wonder if that irony was lost on her mother and grandmother. And when she finished her seventh incantation, and the three of them completed their third circle of the cauldron, the nightfire that burned within blazed twenty feet into the air. It seemed to randomly bounce within the barrier their circling had created, until Medea realized that the flames were bouncing around in the same path that the coven's magics had taken. After thirty seconds of the nightfire's blazing, the flames extinguished themselves, and light seemed to return to the clearing that the intersecting three roads sat in. Expectantly, all three witches looked to the cauldron.

For nearly a minute nothing happened; but then Medea heard it, hissing. Rising from the cauldron came a snake, its scales red, black and white, and it slithered toward Medea's mother. Bringing her left thumb to her mouth, Circe drew it across her teeth, before allowing drops of blood and saliva to fall from her thumb onto the snake's head. "Now you live only to fulfill my vengeance, demon. My words shall lead you to draw blood from those that persecute my family. Failing me, is equal to failing the gods themselves, understand?" As a response, the snake slithered closer to her mother, and then to Medea's slight surprise, up Circe's body. With her enhanced vision, and the fact that her slip was just as translucent as her own, Medea was able to see the demon snake wrap itself around her mother's full breasts in an infinite eight, resting its head in the space between Circe's breasts.

The summoning now over, and having not failed in any way during it, Medea felt confident enough in herself to speak her mind to her elders about the doubts she had of their plan. As Hecate and Circe turned to leave, Medea said, "Mother, Grandmother wait. I wish to speak of our plan." Her mother and grandmother both turned back but did nothing to hide their annoyed expressions. This was nothing new for Medea, who had become accustom to seeing this and other expressions bordering on disgust and disappointment whenever she'd spoken out of late. "I know that you think that we have been treated like less than human since the Empire changed its religion-and I completely agree with that fact, as well as the fact that something needs to be done about it-I'm just not so sure that that something has to be the slaughter of all these people. If we want to change their hearts and minds about the way we live our lives, so that they treat us with the respect we deserve, we shouldn't go about it in a fashion that only will-to them at least-legitimize the way they treat us. I do not think that we should use this demon to kill the monotheists who have taken over the Empire, but rather use him to show them that our faith is as real and as potent as theirs."

For a moment, there was silence and Medea actually hoped that her words had made her mother and grandmother reconsider their plan. But when she heard her mother's distinctive sigh, she knew she'd failed. "Which goddess did I wrong to have such a weak-hearted daughter?" her mother asked of no one.

Having heard this particular taunt before, Medea didn't back down. "It's not weakness that my suggestion shows Mother, but simply a better understanding of human nature. Jupiter knows that I would kill some of the people who torment us for simply practicing our faith; I just don't see how coming across as the monsters they already think we are helps us. Christianity is spreading through the world like wildfire since the Empire converted to it, and those of us able to perform magic are growing smaller and smaller every year. All I'm saying is that, maybe, starting a war isn't the smartest thing to be doing right now. We should try to reconvert some people back to worshipping the gods, not simply kill them all for not doing so."

Medea looked to her grandmother, in hopes that she was convincing her to reconsider the path they'd chosen to take. What she got instead was a hard slap across her face. She didn't know why, but the slap her grandmother gave in response hurt Medea more than just psychically. Being abused by her mother and grandmother like this was nothing new to Medea, but the brief moment of hope that had followed her initial words was what made this slap hurt worse than most.

"Who cares what they think, girl?" her grandmother asked with scorn. "It's not our place to show people the right path of worship; we are the keepers of the mystic powers of Terra and her matriarchy." This statement had been bored into Medea's mind since she could talk, and the fact that her grandmother seemed to think that she still needed to learn this pillar of their faith was insulting to the point of tears. "Besides," her grandmother added with disdain, clearly knowing the effect her words were having on her granddaughter. "When they pray to their god and nothing happens, they'll pray to the gods that they cast aside, the *true* gods, and find results. Save your tears, Medea, for I'm doing what you asked: changing their traitorous hearts back to our gods-I'm just also showing them that their initial lack of faith has dire consequences."

Before Medea could react to Hecate's words, she'd turned away from her granddaughter and disappeared as thunder rolled. Turning to her mother, Medea awaited the berating she knew to be coming silently, willing her eyes to harden and dry of the tears her grandmother's treating of her had caused. "By Jove Medea, you're the greatest disappointment of my life. You crave the love and respect of your coven but you insist on defying it at every opportunity. If you were not a part of this coven, I'd disown you and curse you for your weakness. When will you realize that what your grandmother says is the truth: these people need to pay, not only for what they do to us but for their lack of real faith as well. So, stop your annoying whining and get with the program, you pathetic girl. Or Saturn as my witness, the next time you undermine this coven's plans, I'll slice your throat with a lead sickle myself." And like her mother before her, Medea's mother turned away from Medea and disappeared as thunder rolled.

Enraged by what her mother and grandmother had said, Medea picked up the cauldron that the demon had arisen from, and threw it back on the ground with all her enchanted strength. The force of the throw caused the cauldron to break, as a section holding one of the legs was broken off from the rest of the cauldron. With an annoyed sigh, she picked up both pieces and whispered a quick mending spell that caused the cauldron to fix itself. "One day Mother, you will realize how much you need me, and when you're counting on me, I just might fail to live up to your hopes for me. And you'll have nobody to blame but yourself for not having any faith in me." *I am NOT pathetic!* She thought to herself.

But as she walked away, nearly naked and holding the cauldron to herself, Medea felt the slightest doubt at that statement's truthfulness.

Chapter 3
Juba

The heat of the midmorning sun, while slightly lessened by the intermittent clouds, was a welcomed reprieve from the unusual cold of the autumn in Juba's mind. As he went about his duties as the servant of the Iracundus household, Juba once again thanked God for giving him a master like Marcus. Many masters of the slaves he saw on a daily basis were not always as kind or tolerant as his could be. Juba had long ago accepted the fact that he was a slave; after being taken from his home by a battalion of Roman soldiers when he was just entering his twentieth year. Now, twenty years later, Juba had plenty to be thankful for and one of the highest on that list was the privilege to be considered a friend to his master: Marcus Iracundus.

Today, Juba's duties were fairly easy. He was to collect a few household supplies and ingredients for Bathsheba and Mary's, Marcus' wife and daughter respectively, monthly teas, and then watch Gabriel and Marcus II as their father preached in the square. This was especially easy as both boys were quite well behaved. Gabriel, the elder of the two sons, would often spend his time within town in the library reading the epic poems of Homer, Virgil and Hesiod; the boy was rarely without a scroll in his hand or belt. Marcus II, who was barely ten years into life, spent most of the time his father preached sitting on a vacant crate with a bored expression on his face. Most of the time, Juba would be hounded by silly requests from the boy to help him pass the time.

Having seen Gabriel to the library safely, and Marcus II staying with his father for the time being, Juba went to the market square to fetch everything his master had tasked him with collecting. His first stop was a vendor that sold the cloth that the women made into clothes. The vendor, a woman named Meredith, greeted Juba with a warm smile and quickly cut the lengths of cloth he requested. Before he left her hut, Juba noticed a roll of green fabric sitting in the corner of the shop.

Noticing his attention on the fabric, Meredith asked, "Pretty, isn't it? The green. Would you like some, for your wife perhaps?" She'd come around and held the fabric up for Juba to inspect.

"Oh, no, I am not married. But it is very pretty, yes." Juba responded. Reaching out and running a hand over it, Juba felt the soft fabric. "It is very soft, too."

"Yes, it is. But sadly, not many people want to buy it; and it is expensive. I've had this roll since I first opened and have only ever sold two dresses worth. But I'm curious, if you're not married, what about this fabric caught your eye?"

"My master, he loves that color. And next month is his and his wife's marriage anniversary," Juba explained as he looked at the vendor. Noting that she seemed to be somewhere between ten and fifteen years older than him, Juba clarified further, "I thought that having her make a dress in his favorite color would be a great way for my mistress to show her love for my master. But I do not have enough to pay for the material and get everything else that I am to get today."

"Ah, I see," Meredith said, as she went to put the fabric back in its corner. But as she was about to set it down, she turned back to Juba. "Maybe we can make a deal, Juba. I'll give you enough of this lovely green fabric for your mistress to make a dress at half the price that I would normally sell it, but you need to do a couple of things for me." Unsure, but intrigued by her offer, Juba gave Meredith a quizzical look. "First, whenever your master or mistress need fabric for anything, I'd like your business." This seemed a reasonable concession to Juba so he nodded his acceptance. Smiling, Meredith gave her second condition, "Second, meet me here two hours after sun down."

When the vendor winked at him, Juba actually felt his cheeks warm at the suggestion. It had been a while since he had been with a woman in such a fashion, but he had felt himself longing for such an encounter over the past few months. Flashing a bright smile, made brighter by its contrast to his dark skin, Juba winked back at the fabric vendor as he pulled another coin from the pouch on his belt.

Twenty minutes later, Juba was returning to the part of the market where Marcus had set up his preaching stand, having finished the rest of his shopping. His master was clearly in the middle of his preaching if the look on his son's bored face was any indication. And judging by the crowd that seemed to grow every few minutes as more and more people came to hear the word of the Empire's new religion, his master had been preaching for about twenty minutes.

As Juba made his way over to where Marcus II was sitting, he bumped into a man wearing a long-hooded cloak. The man turned to see who had bumped him, his face was hidden by his cloak's large hood. Before Juba could excuse himself, the man grabbed his arm and squeezed it tightly. "Juba, I know you made a promise, but you must stay home tonight! Something is not right; something is wrong with Terra in this town. It's not safe tonight. Stay home!"

Juba was slightly unnerved by what this stranger had said: on the one hand, there was no way this man could have known Juba's name or his new plans for the evening. But on the other hand, the things he said made no sense. And this man was clearly a heathen, based on his use of the name 'Terra' for the world; and his master Marcus had always said that heathens were never to be trusted. Pulling his arm free from the man's tight grip, Juba simply said, "I apologize for hitting you sir." Before things could get any weirder, Juba continued his trek to Marcus II.

But before Juba could make it to Marcus II, something at the edge of the market caught his eye. It was the daughter of his master, Mary, making her way into one of the shops, unsupervised. Marcus had made it clear on many occasions that Mary, mainly due to her overly sinful nature, was never to go anywhere unsupervised. Heaving a sigh at the trouble that this would undoubtedly cause this evening at supper, Juba took a quick glance at Marcus II, saw that he was still sitting alone, and altered course for the shop Mary had entered.

When he realized that the shop was one of the jewel vendors that the square offered, Juba had an aching suspicion of what his young mistress was up to. Peaking his head in, Juba saw that only Mary and the shop owners were inside. The shop owners were a young attractive couple, clearly married, and clearly absorbed with whatever Mary was saying to them. Stepping in quietly to hear and see what happened more clearly, Juba slowly inched himself closer to the three young people.

Mary, who nobody could mistake for anyone's daughter but her mother's, was standing behind the female vendor and talking to both in a low voice that Juba hoped would be similar to the one he'd hear from Meredith later that evening. "…n't afford them, but I've always loved pearls. Having those white pools wrapped around my neck, dipping into the edge of my dress," here she paused as she drew a finger along the curve of the woman's breasts, and drawing her husband's focus to the valley between them. "I'd feel just so classy with a pearl necklace, wouldn't you?" she asked the woman as her hand travelled lower still from the vendor's breasts. Juba was quite taken aback by Mary's brazen and public sinfulness, until he saw her other hand about to pocket a pair of gold and ruby earrings.

Despite the fact that she was stealing, Juba had to begrudgingly compliment Mary on her skill in the art of distraction. How she was able to enrapture not only the man, but the woman as well (as well as using her to keep the man's focus elsewhere) was quite masterful, for one as young as Mary, who being Gabriel's twin, was barely in her twentieth year. Pushing past his reluctant praise of Mary, and her talents for thieving, Juba rushed up to the three other people in the shop as if he'd just come in from outside. Giving a slight huff to sell the charade he was about to perform, Juba saw Mary's face slightly pale as she recognized him. "Ah, here you are, Mary. Your father has been looking for you for half an hour; we should go and make sure he does not buy anything that your mother would be upset to find out about." Grabbing her hand that held the earrings, Juba started to drag her outside as he slyly took the jewelry from her hand. Accidently on purposely running himself into a table, Juba dropped the earrings into a wooden bowl filled with other fine pieces in it. "So sorry to have wasted your time, but we must really be going now." And with that, the two of them were outside.

Juba was surprised, but extremely grateful, that Mary had not said anything during the entire ordeal. But it also made him suspicious of why she went along with everything, as she would always try to usurp her parents' authority in a situation like this. "You need to go home, Mary. Your father does not like when you are out alone; and if he knew what you were doing inside… he would disown you again. Please do not make me have to tell him and just do as you are asked."

Throughout his pleading for her to do what was best for her, Mary had a smile on her face that was quite mischievous. After a brief pause, where she seemed to be taking in his reaction, Mary finally responded. "Ok, Juba, I'll go home without a fuss." This statement actually made Juba smile. "But I want you to answer two simple questions before I go." That statement made Juba's smile falter. "First, why didn't you tell them about the earrings? And second, did you enjoy the show?"

Sighing internally, Juba shook his head. But before Mary could react to his reaction to her questions, he answered her. "I did not inform that nice couple about your attempt to steal from them because I did not want to get you in trouble. As for the show, as you call it," Juba noted that Mary's expression became keener at the mention of her show, indicating that she was truly interested in his opinion. "As for your show, you were quite…mesmerizing. Were you not using your gifts to break one of God's sacred commandments, your father may have even been proud of you. The two of you are more alike than I think either of you knows. I know that if you were to use your way with words, to inspire piety and not theft, your family would love you all the more."

"Don't ruin this for me, Juba," Mary teased.

"I simply want what is best for you, Miss Mary," he replied, letting his hand caress her cheek briefly. "Now, please, do as I have asked and return home, before your father sees you out of the house." Giving her a meaningful look, Juba saw that Mary would comply.

"Alright, Juba, I'll go. But I think you should be more worried about my brother than me at the moment. If I'm not mistaken, that's the witch from the outskirts of town that's taking to him." Her smile was playful, making Juba think it was a ploy to distract him.

But as he turned to indulge her, he indeed saw that there was a woman talking with the youngest Iracundus. Momentarily forgetting about Mary, Juba made his way to Marcus II. His heart beat slightly faster in his chest as he indeed recognized the woman talking with the boy as one of the witches from the edge of town. Racing over to the boy, Juba caught the end of whatever it was they were talking about.

"…sk and you'll be rewarded," the witch was saying. Juba was relieved to see Marcus II walk away from the woman.

"I do not wish to be rude, miss, but the boy's father would not appreciate the fact you were talking to him, given the fact that you do not share the faith in Christ as our savior." Juba didn't want to insult the witch; while his master didn't believe in their powers, he knew first-hand how powerful this woman could be.

"It is not your rudeness that would bother me," the woman said. Her blue eyes were cold, as if she had no love in her heart. "But fret not, dutiful servant, I was simply asking the boy to explain his father's faith to me. That is the boy's father, and your master, preaching isn't it?" the woman asked, indicating Marcus as he stood on a crate.

"It is," Juba said. "Now, if you will excuse me, I must return to him for he is almost finished for the day. Good day, Madam," he said with a slight bow of his head, still trying to avoid the woman's wrath.

Turning in the same direction as his young charge had fled, Juba escaped the witch as he made his way toward both Marcus Iracundus'. But it was when he saw the younger Marcus that Juba noticed that the boy seemed to be being accosted by the same heathen that had so unnerved Juba as he finished his errands. Picking up his pace so as to protect his young master, Juba saw the man look at him.

Suddenly there was a crash of thunder from above. As it was a perfectly nice day, the clouds nowhere near dark enough to conceal thunder, everyone turned to the sky in search of its source. And in the ensuing moment of confusion, Juba lost sight of the heathen that was the source of his current panic. But upon seeing Marcus II being picked up by his father in a loving embrace, Juba felt himself relax; the boy was safe with his father, and it was time to return home. Reuniting with his masters, the three of them set out for the library to find young Gabriel and return to their home at the edge of town.

Chapter 4
The Reluctant Learner

While she always tried to pay attention to every lesson her mother and grandmother taught her about the various magical properties of everything around her, Medea could not even feign interest in today's lesson. Although the past month and a half had been focused on perfecting the summoning ritual they'd performed the previous night, today had seen a return to her previous area of study: sex magic. And while that had made Medea uncomfortable enough to learn, today's lesson on the magical potency of semen was especially hard to engage with.

"Of course, like with everything else that Terra gives us, the freshness of the semen will add to its strength in your spells. That is why, when the time comes in the next year, you will need to use the spell I'm about to tell you, with semen directly from the source."

Medea couldn't hide the disgust that crawled across her face as Hecate told her that she would need to not only use semen in a spell within a year, but that it would also have to be fresh from the source. Medea had always known that she would be called upon to birth the next generation into their coven, but she never knew that it would have to be so soon.

And while girls her age all around her were married and having children, Medea hadn't even found a boy she liked enough to consider taking to her bed to conceive her daughter.

"Don't give me that look of disgust, girl!" her grandmother barked when she saw the look on her face. "Sex magic is one of our most powerful and ancient forms of magic, taught to us by Trivia herself! You dare scoff at our greatest tradition! I'll teach you!" And with a speed and dexterity that of someone much younger, her grandmother stood from her seat, grabbed Medea by the hair and pulled her around the table. Standing herself to her full height, being taller than Medea herself, Hecate cut an opposing figure from her granddaughter's current vantage point of her knees. "You are such a disappointment, Medea." *Slap!* "In all my years teaching your mother, she was never so uninterested or so unnerved by what me and my mother taught her. But you" *Slap!* "you have the audacity" *Slap!* "to be disgusted by the oldest aspect of our craft! An ancient art that was taught to us by the goddess Herself!" Here is where her grandmother slapped her twice, one on each cheek.

But just before her grandmother could continue her verbal assault, a clash of thunder announced the return of her mother from the market. But what surprised Medea was how the previously calm day seemed to grow more chaotic as the wind blew harder and harder. Clearly her mother was upset about something.

But the wind immediately died as her mother walked through the door into their home. "It's done," she said simply while trying to head to the door to their joint bedroom.

"Circe!" her grandmother called, stopping Medea's mother in her tracks. Carelessly tossing aside Medea, her grandmother walked to her daughter with a measured step. "What aren't you telling us, Circe?" Medea had heard that deadly calm in her grandmother's voice before, and it never boded well.

Even from the other side of the room, Medea could hear her mother's gulp as she swallowed her fear. "Someone-someone who can stop the demon-knows what I did. And I think they warned the servant of the family."

In the silence that followed her mother's admission, Medea felt the slightest sliver of hope. Maybe with this complication to their plan, her mother and grandmother would reconsider the alternative she'd suggested the night before. But that thought was immediately quashed by her grandmother's next words.

"And why didn't you simply kill this person and servant? You're constantly telling me that you're willing to do whatever it takes to please me, Circe; so why did you allow for this threat to our revenge to remain? Even your worthless daughter would have known that removing such a threat was necessary before she returned to this house!" Hecate's voice had gotten louder the more she accused her daughter.

But unlike herself a moment earlier, Medea's mother did not crumble under the death glare of the family matriarch. "I couldn't kill him, mother. As much as I wanted to, it isn't my place to kill him."

Upon hearing her defense, Medea's grandmother slapped her mother across the face. "Idiotic girl! You are a witch, in possession of the most ancient and potent of magics at your disposal! Who could be so powerful as to warrant not only your refusal, but abdication of the right to kill this one man?"

The look of wrath in her grandmother's eyes was so potent that Medea could feel its heat, even with her grandmother completely turned away from her. But when her mother looked away from her own mother to look on Medea, Medea felt her blood freeze in fear. In her mother's eyes Medea only saw contempt as she said the single word, "Him." But oddly, she felt this contempt was not meant for her for once.

And when her grandmother joined her mother in looking upon her, Medea's fear increased sevenfold. But seeing the calm, bordering on malevolent joy, in her grandmother's eyes, had Medea find her voice. "Who is it? Who is so powerful as to allow the great Hecate to ignore a huge failure be committed by her own daughter?" Medea strangely hoped her disrespectful tone would anger one of her two elders to answer her question.

Instead, all her grandmother did was give a small smile and turn toward the bedroom that the three of them shared. Medea, while confused by this turn of events, didn't need her mother's silent motioning for her to follow her grandmother into the bedroom. Upon entering, Medea noticed her grandmother kneeling on the floor, a piece of the floor at her side. When she stood the next moment and turned toward her daughter and granddaughter, Hecate had a bronze handled lead sickle and a silver ring with a jewel made of onyx at its center. And with that same small smile on her lips, she placed both the sickle and the ring into Medea's hand. "Congratulations granddaughter; you get to kill two birds with one stone. Failing in this isn't possible for I will personally kill you should you do so." And without another word, her grandmother left the room and shut the door, leaving Medea alone with her mother.

When Circe gently grabbed Medea's hand and pulled her to the bed, she gave a confused look to her mother's gentleness. "I know you're confused my dear, but the time has come for two of your longest held questions to be answered," her mother told her in a tone Medea only had the faintest memory of her ever using.

"Yes, I'm confused. First of all, you-you mother-are being *nice* to me! You've not shown me any kindness since I was six. Secondly, who in all of Tartarus is 'Him' and why isn't grandmother upset anymore that you didn't kill him? And what did she mean that I now could kill two birds with one stone? What's going on?" She didn't know when she did it, but at some point during her questioning, Medea had gotten off the bed and started to pace. When she'd finished talking and found herself leveling the lead sickle at her mother, a twinge of fear ran up the girl's spine.

But with uncharacteristic calmness, her mother simply lowered the sickle leveled at her and then patted the spot beside her that Medea had just vacated. "Sit Medea, and I will explain everything." Tentatively, and slightly alarmed by her mother's calm and gentle demeanor, Medea sat at her side "I know that you won't believe me when I say this Medea, but I love you. I know that my words and actions don't always-if ever-reflect that, but it is true. And while I may not have been nice to you since you were six, please let me give you some of the motherly love that you've always wanted in this moment.

"What I'm about to tell you, is going to upset you. You're probably going to be more upset than I was when this day came for me. But the reason your grandmother isn't mad that I didn't kill the man that knows about the demon is because you are supposed to kill him. Since before you were even conceived, he has been yours, and yours alone, to kill."

Looking to her mother, Medea couldn't hide her confusion. "What do you mean?" There were so many ways that Medea meant that question. What did she mean that this news would upset her, even more than it had upset her mother when she had been told it? Why was it Medea's duty to kill this stranger? And, most pressingly, what did her mother mean she loved her?

"You've wondered how it is that me and your grandmother have more power than you, how magic is easier for us than yourself. Killing this man, in the manner which I'm about to tell you, will level the playing field and you'll be as powerful as the two of us; and our coven will be at its most powerful. But to accomplish this, you need to do exactly what I tell you by tomorrow night at midnight. If you don't, not only will your magic fade, but all of our magic will fade, and nobody wants that to happen. Do you understand?"

The earnest plea and longing in her mother's eyes brought the acceptance of this out of Medea. And as she cautiously nodded her head, she saw her mother give her a genuinely happy smile. “Ok, now to complete this ritual you’re going to need to do these three things.”

Chapter 5
Gabriel

Upon his return home from the library earlier that afternoon, Gabriel Iracundus had eaten a well sized lunch. And while he had enjoyed the unusual quiet from both of his siblings, he thought nothing of it as he took up his favorite reading nook in the family's front yard. Having returned home from the library with a copy of his favorite section of Homer's Iliad, the young man readjusted the small knife in his belt that he always kept on his person for protection and began to read.

He was just getting to his favorite part, the battle between Achilles and Penthesilea and their oddly romantic connection, when he heard the distinctive giggle of his mother coming from down the street. Setting his scroll down, he stood up and walked to the gateway to their home to greet his mother as she returned home. Looking up and down the street to see his mother, Gabriel spotted her leaving the home of their new neighbor Julius Captus.

Julius had moved next door to the Iracundus family after the untimely death of his wife last year, and Gabriel's mother had taken it upon herself to not only make him feel welcome in the new neighborhood, but also try to soothe his ailing heart. Gabriel was extremely proud of his mother for her efforts to help their grieving neighbor, and would often ask how the man was when his mother returned from visiting him. But today was the first time that, as he watched his mother return, Gabriel noticed a strange look overcome Julius' face as he watched his neighbor leave. It was a look that his father had often berated his sister for giving off whenever she was allowed to go into town with them: greedy lust.

But before Gabriel could think about it for too much, the look disappeared to one of general happiness before he returned to his home. Turning his attention back to his mother as she arrived at the clearing in the wall where Gabriel awaited her, the boy gave his mother a hug. "From the giggle you gave as you left and the smile on his face, I'd say that your efforts to heal his broken heart are really starting to bear fruit, Mother."

His mother stiffened the slightest bit as she returned his hug before releasing him. "Death and heartache are hard things to overcome, Gabriel. Especially with someone as young as Julius. But yes, he's been very open to my attempts to help him move on from the death of his wife. But with all that said, it has been a hard day, and this heat is making me uncomfortable; I think I'm going to take a bath and wash it all away." And with a kiss to his cheek, his mother returned to the house as Gabriel returned to his nook and scroll.

He was just settling himself into the nook when he heard footsteps approaching. Thinking it was one of his siblings come to pester him for whatever reason, Gabriel didn't bother to look up. "Can I not go one day where I get to read in peace?" he asked absently, hoping to fend off whichever of his siblings was ruining his solitude.

"Pray that your siblings survive, for you'll miss their pestering you more than you know when they're gone," a voice that Gabriel didn't recognize said in an ominous tone.

Dropping his scroll and drawing the small knife on his belt, Gabriel found himself standing before a tall man in a long, hooded, blue cloak. He held his hands in the opposite sleeves, but upon seeing the knife he raised them over his head. "Who are you and what are you doing here?"

"I'm not a threat, Gabriel. I simply wish to warn you, as I tried to warn your family's servant Juba in the market. Your town's coven of witches have cursed your brother. And in so doing they have cursed the very earth itsel—"

"There's no such thing as curses!" Gabriel stated. "And my brother certainly isn't cursed! Now, before I hurt you, I ask again: who are you and what are you doing here?"

Finally lowering his hands, the man returned them to their sleeves. Stepping forward slightly he said, "Do not be so dismissive of the magic that those women hold. My power cannot help you, only their deaths can save you. Like I said, I'm simply here to help you." Then he took a quick look at the scroll lying on the ground. "I know that my time has come, please don't make me more of a Cassandra. Heed my warnings!"

Before Gabriel could react, the stranger had raised his cloak's hood and leapt over the stone wall that surrounded the Iracundus home. He was about to run after the man when the sound of his brother's voice called his attention back to the house. "Gabriel, Father wants you to come help Juba prepare dinner." Gazing upon his younger brother in the doorway, Gabriel dismissed the ravings of the stranger. Curses weren't real and his brother seemed perfectly fine.

Sheathing his knife and picking up his discarded scroll, Gabriel returned to the house. Tousling his brother's sandy curls, he led the way into the kitchen to help prepare the family's supper for the evening.

Chapter 6
The Demon

I was so happy when my Goddess chose me to help the witches enact their revenge. It seems both an eternity and no time at all since I last felt the pulse of life leave the helpless victims of my sickness. And to now be given the chance to feel it once again (at the behest of those in servitude to my Goddess) was the greatest gift I could have asked for in death. Sadly, this serpentine body does not give me the ability to take life itself, so I must make do with the horror and revulsion those I possess feel as I relish the blood flowing through their fingers.

My earthly Mistress had instructed me to wait until the night and to not only terrorize the family of the boy she'd had me originally possess, but also this town. So, it was a great surprise, when I slither into the daughter's bedroom to find her sneaking off to an orgy in a clearing in the forest on the outskirts of town. To ensure the maximum carnage and terror, I wait until the orgy is in full swing.

One by one, I possess those at the edge of the clearing, feeling them rip their lovers' hearts out. Their cries of pain and anguish mix with those unawares' cries of ecstasy. I'm ever so slowly making my way to the girl; fittingly enough, she's in the center of this congregation of lust. And blessed Hestia, look at her inhale the cock on that DONKEY! It's almost a shame to have to kill such talent and lust. But…to spread terror, some of these people should live.

I've finally reached her. Her lust is nearly overwhelming, but nothing can sate my own lust, bloodlust. Taking a rock, I knock out the man she is now practically assaulting with the ferocity of her hips. And now, I live once again!

While I was quite prolific when I was alive, I never killed so many in a single area in such quick succession. I prefer to enjoy my hunt, almost tasting the fear in the air as my victims ran from me. And while tonight has plenty of fear in the air, speed is my greatest asset to spread fear. In all of five minutes it's over. The girl is covered in blood, I've left five survivors to spread word into town, and my main victim has a heart in each hand as she lies unconscious on the ground in the center of this visceral ode to my bloodlust and tribute to the great Hecate.

My nightly work finished, I slither home, to the boy I will make kill his family.

Chapter 7
The Distraught Daughter

Medea could feel the draw the spell her and her mother had cast upon her grow stronger and stronger the deeper into town she went. Finally finding herself standing before a building that, at least according to her mother, was once a temple to the goddess Proserpina. The temple was now abandoned, which suited Medea's purposes fine; she didn't want to be seen doing these things.

Her mother had been right, Medea was horrified and revolted by the things her mother told her to do. And to this man, a man she'd longed for her whole life. How fitting that all this was to take place in a temple to a goddess of fertility and death; a contradiction as oxymoronic as her tasks this night.

Did he know that she was coming? Did he even know who she was; who they were to each other? For the first time in her life, Medea was actually grateful for the lack of any knowledge or connection with her soon to be victim. Their absence would make this easier.

As she neared the abandoned temple, Medea saw the flicker of a small fire inside that signaled to her that he was indeed inside the temple. Quietly as she could, Medea snuck into the temple, trying to take stock of the situation, before announcing her presence. The man was seated with his back to her around the fire she'd seen from the outside, a rabbit roasting over top of it.

"I appreciate and respect your need to be stealthy, but if it's all the same to you, I would like for you to sit and talk with me before you kill me, my dear." The man's voice was gentle, but deep. And he almost seemed weary, like he knew today was coming for a long time and that he had accepted his fate a long time ago.

But despite his calm, his knowing that she was there unsettled Medea slightly. Walking around to sit opposite him at the fire, she kept her face a mask while trying to map it over his. But she had always looked too much like her mother to be able to play that game. Not to mention it was pointless to try to make any connections with him if she wanted this to be an emotionless affair.

"How did you know I was there? Me and my mother put a secrecy spell on me when I left; nobody should have been able to detect my presence." Her voice was even and she didn't break eye contact with him, but inside her fear and uncertainty were raging in her head urging her to break down and cry.

"Surely, you can figure that out. Your mother has always felt that those with magic were superior to those without; it's not too big a leap to think that she would try to find a man who has magic to father a daughter with." So, he did know who she was and who they were to each other. "I'm sorry that you've lived your life without knowing me. I've only known who you are for the past year, despite knowing this day was coming since before I met your mother. I've spent the last year searching for you, hoping in vain, that I could change the future. But it would appear that I've only brought it to bear."

"I'm not just here to kill you father," Medea said, as her calm facade finally cracked with the escape of a tear. "There's so much more to tonight than your death." Unable to bear the weight of her intended actions, Medea was finally forced to look away from her father.

But even as she looked away, Medea saw the confusion that crossed his face at her revelation. "For nearly as long as I've had the visions of this night, I've been confused by the fact that you needed two cuts to kill me. When I realized that it was you who was the one to kill me, I figured it was due to the fact that you would hesitate to kill me and need a second cut to do it right. Why do I now feel that that assumption is wrong?"

"Because, the first cut isn't meant to kill you. Should I wish it, the first cut doesn't even need to really be that damaging. I've cut men's throats before, and yes the first time I did need a second opportunity to get it right, but I'll only need one cut to end your life tonight." As she said this, Medea glared at her father in anger; as if it was his fault and not her mother's and grandmother's for forcing her to kill those people over the past six years.

It was the first time that he had taken his eyes off her since she'd come into the firelight. But it wasn't to avoid her gaze that accused him of abandoning her, it was to check the rabbit that sat cooking over the fire. Once he'd turned it over, he turned his attention back to her. "What's your name? If you're going to kill me, and since you are my daughter, I think I deserve to at least know your name."

Medea sat and studied her father for a long moment before she finally answered him. “Medea, my name is Medea.” It was an even longer moment before she asked, “What’s yours?”

“Lucius,” he said after a brief moment. An awkward silence fell between them after they’d revealed their names, that her father finally broke with the question she had thought he’d asked instead of asking for her name. “What sort of spell do you need my blood for, considering you apparently can’t use the outflow from when you slit my throat?”

Despite telling herself that she could be clinical about this part of her task, Medea felt herself blush at the answer to his question. She hoped that the firelight hid the reddening of her cheeks, as she forced herself to keep eye contact and a blank face. “It’s a divination spell meant to show me the father of my child,” she said as evenly as possible.

“What aren’t you telling me, Medea?” he asked with a searching look upon his face. “Mixing divination and fertility magic is complicated, dangerous and unpredictable. And it certainly would require more than just my blood.” He gazed at her with a most penetrating look as he sought the answers on her face. “What else do you need, and do you know if you can even perform such a spell?”

Not faltering from his gaze, Medea kept her eyes steady as she gave her father a slightly glaring look. “I do not think it appropriate for you to judge my abilities. I’ve been trained in the art of magic since birth. I may have just learned the spell I’m about to perform earlier today, but despite your concerns, it’s actually quite simple. If a little awkward.” As she finished, Medea couldn't continue to look him in the eye.

"Forgive me, daughter, I didn't mean to imply that you didn't know how to or couldn't cast this spell. As strange as it may seem, I was only concerned for your safety. And what's so awkward about this spell?"

Steeling herself to what she knew she had to do, Medea took a deep breath with closed eyes. As she exhaled, and her eyes opened, Medea looked upon her father as she stood up. "Stand up," she commanded as she gestured with the lead sickle in her hand. Once he'd complied and come to stand in front of her, Medea finally let her emotions free.

Throwing her arms around him, she hugged herself tight to him as a flood of tears flowed from her eyes. "Forgive me, Daddy," she said. When she felt his arms wrap around her, a tremor spasmed through her body. "I've longed to know you for the past eighteen years! And now to have you finally here, I can't stand to look at you! But for my coven and my daughter, I must do this." Pushing herself back, Medea lowered the straps on her dress before letting it fall to the floor, leaving her naked to her father's eyes.

Before he could let out a gasp of surprise at her actions, Medea was already on her knees and pulling at his robe. Grabbing hold of his manhood tightly through the remaining layers of clothing, Medea heard her father give a small moan of pain. Loosening her grip slightly, she looked up into his eyes. "No questions, and your being relaxed will make this go much easier, Lucius." Her use of his name was meant as a final mental bastion for this being clinical, and not erotic, in nature.

"Ok," was his reply in a weak voice. Summoning the last of her courage, and holding it in her throat, Medea started to once again remove her father's manhood from his robes.

Once she had fished it out, she once again looked into her father's eyes. "These are your last moments, Lucius; you should enjoy them. Most men would love the opportunity to die with a naked woman before them with their cock her mouth." Again, without waiting for his reply, Medea refocused on the task both at and in hand and lowered her mouth to her father's cock. Her mother had warned her that the awkwardness of the situation may prohibit her father from initially responding favorably, but that no man could resist the temptation of a willing mouth. And so, Medea put the few tips her mother had offered to help accelerate things along into use.

It seemed her mother had taught her well, as in less than three minutes her father's cock had grown inside her mouth to the point where it hurt her jaw as she tried to swallow it. Pulling herself off for a moment to once again engage in conversation, she looked up into his eyes. "I'm not sure if this is an impressive cock or not, Daddy, but I'm going to assume it is. It's thick and strong, and the liquid leaking out of it is more agreeable than I thought it would be." Giving it a few more sucks, Medea turned back to her father once again. "Let me know when you're about to finish."

As she returned to sucking on him, she heard him give an approving moan. "Jupiter's cock, Medea, you're not going to have to wait long," he groaned between deep breaths. And he was right; in five minutes her father was moaning quite audibly, and Medea felt him grow even bigger in her mouth. "My gods, Medea! I'm about to-to—"

Spitting him out, Medea grabbed the lead sickle that she'd left at her knees, and before he could even begin to stop her, she sliced her left palm as well as his manhood. The pain brought on by her cut seemed to be the final piece for him to achieve orgasm, for he erupted as soon as the blade touched his skin.

Grabbing a hold of his firing member, Medea jacked her left hand up and down his shaft as she aimed the spurts of his semen onto her stomach. Once he'd finished, Medea took her left hand, now covered in both of their blood, and used it to rub the mess on her stomach in circles, switching directions on every third rotation. "*Seed of my seeder, blood of father and daughter, show me the one who is my breeder,*" she chanted as she rubbed the mixture into her skin.

Her father had collapsed back to the ground with a look of utter disbelief on his face, but Medea was able to read the pleasure that radiated off him. As she felt the blood and semen on her hand began to dry, Medea's vision began to cloud over. As she finished rubbing a set of three circles, everything went black. But something shifted in the darkness; Medea squinted at the image, barely making out the silhouette of a face. But before any clarity over what the father of her child was supposed to look like could be discerned, her vision cleared and she was once again staring at the form of her father, who was still recovering from what she'd done to him.

Medea couldn't believe it, she'd not failed in her task, but the answer she'd sought had not come. Her mother had told her that, should she perform the spell correctly, the vision of who the father of her daughter would be would cloud her mind and become clear as the sunrise. While her vision had clouded over, no clarity had come.

Startled out of her contemplations by the sound of the sickle dropping out of her hand, Medea looked down to it without truly seeing it for a long moment. The sound of her father coming back to his senses brought her attention back to him for a brief moment, as she watched him return his manhood to the inside of his robes. Picking up the sickle, Medea walked over to her father, gripping and re-gripping the weapon in her hand.

Her half failure had made her numb to the world. Kneeling down at her father's side, she waited until his eyes came to focus on her. Raising the sickle to his throat, Medea saw the flicker of fear that crossed his face. "I'm sorry, Daddy," was all she said before she slit his throat. At any other moment in time, the regret and pain in Lucius' eyes would have caused her own to fill with tears. But the knowledge-or more accurately lack of knowledge-in her head consumed all thoughts in her head.

All thoughts, except the spell that would allow her to have a greater and easier access to magic. "*O Terra, giver of all things, I offer the blood of he who gave me life. Grant me, O Terra, greater access to the powers you gave me at birth. By Trivia, the goddess of night and magic, I implore your favor!*"

And as she watched the ground drink away her father's lifeblood, Medea felt an impact on the air within her chest. And she finally felt the rush of power that her mother and grandmother had been promising her would come for as long as she could remember.

But this only served to cause more tears to fall from her eyes. Standing back up, Medea walked back to where her dress lay strewn on the ground. Grabbing it and hugging it to herself, Medea cried out in anguish as the weight of the night fell upon her.

Chapter 8
The Honorable Son

Gabriel sat around the table with his brother at his side and his parents across from him. The empty seat on his other side was meant for his sister, but it was clear that she'd gone out the previous night to do God knows what. It wasn't the first time his twin had escaped the confines of their home to engage in sinful behavior. But apart from the frown his parents gave upon noticing her absence, Mary's lack of presence went unmentioned.

As Juba set down plates with the day's breakfast of eggs and leftover steak in front of first his mother and father, and then his brother and self, Gabriel let thoughts of his sister leave his mind. After having a bite and finding the food, as always, delicious, Gabriel gave an appreciative moan and turned to the family's servant. "Father in Heaven, Juba! You're cooking never ceases to impress me and my stomach. I thank God every day for the events that led you to become a member of this family. Heaven knows that mother and father can't cook this well." This last statement was met with snickers from his brother and mother.

His father on the other hand, was not pleased. "Gabriel!" This brought an end to the snickering. "While I commend you on your manners, it is Juba's job to cook delicious meals for us. The fact that he's able to give you something you enjoy, is simply a part of his duties in service to this family. There's no need to break the fourth Commandment to express your approval of a servant doing his duties."

"Now Marcus," his mother said, "there's no need to reprimand the boy, for saying what is true. Juba is a better cook than either of us could hope to be, and our son is right in recognizing that fact. Gabriel didn't break the fourth Commandment; his comparison wasn't made maliciously, but simply as if saying your robes are my least favorite color on you. My acknowledging that I don't like you in red isn't disrespectful, but merely me expressing my opinion. Gabriel was doing the same thing."

"Yes father. I'm sorry that the way I said what I did came across as disrespectful; I was simply trying to acknowledge Juba's culinary talents. You know that I would never purposefully insult you or mother."

"Very well," his father said after a long pause. "I will acknowledge that you didn't mean your words to be disrespectful. And what you said is true, Juba is a better cook than me or your mother. But let this be a lesson for you Gabriel, as well as for you Marcus: your intentions might not always be clear and words can be misleading. People might take offense to what you say, even if you never meant any." As he finished, both boys nodded their understanding to the lesson their father was trying to impart. "And do you really not like me in red, Bathsheba?"

Giving him a small smile, his mother shook her head. "It was a simple example to illustrate my point, darling.

Truthfully, I care not for what you wear. Now, finish your plate; we wouldn't want Juba to think that he isn't a good cook."

His father smiled at his wife's words, before returning to his breakfast. And as Juba took both his and his brother's plates, the family's servant leaned down and whispered in Gabriel's ear. "I appreciate the compliment, Master Gabriel, but it is an honor just to serve." Gabriel simply nodded his understanding to his words and acknowledgement.

The next few moments were spent in peaceful silence as his parents finished their food. But at the sound of the door opening and shutting, a look of great anger overcame both of his parents' faces. "Mary Iracundus! Come here at once, before I throw you back out onto the streets you enjoy walking so much!" his father yelled toward the front door.

Gabriel saw everyone tense slightly as they awaited Mary's retort to her father's words. But when no words came, and no footsteps could be heard on the stairs, everyone's eyes turned to the doorway that led into the dining room. And what they saw was terrifying.

There was his sister, his twin, looking like all life had left her. The dress she wore was clearly not her own for it was way too big on her skinny frame. Her arms were coated in dried blood from her fingers to just above her elbows. Her usually straight hair was a tangled mess and seemed to have a tinge of red to its normal black luster. Her blue eyes looked out toward them but seemed to see nothing around her. And her mouth was covered in so much blood, Gabriel was surprised she could open it at all.

For the first time in nearly a decade, Gabriel felt the ethereal pull of his twin. The calling they'd always had for each other in their youth, but that had seemed to vanish in the time since their brother was born. There was a rush toward Mary as everyone ran to comfort her. Their mother got to her first and Mary threw her arms around her and began to cry. Gabriel was right behind his mother and he threw his arms around his sister, trying to send thoughts of comfort over the calling that had re-established itself in the past few seconds.

"Mary, sweetheart, what happened? Why are you covered in blood?" her mother asked as she held Mary's head in her hands so that they looked into each other's eyes. But Mary simply buried her head into her mother's chest. His mother stroked her daughter's hair as she cooed in her ear reassurances of Mary's safety and that everything would be alright.

Juba brought a wet cloth and handed it to Gabriel's mother. Taking it, his mother began to wipe the blood away from Mary's mouth. "I will start filling the tub with warm water," he said softly as he left the room to do just that.

Making their way back over to the table, their mother sat Mary down in the seat that their father usually occupied. As his mother continued to wipe the blood away, Gabriel knelt down at his sister's side and took her hand in his. Mary jolted at having his hand in hers, but he simply held her tighter. "Is any of this yours? Are you alright?" he asked as her gazed finally seemed to take him in.

Shaking her head, Mary replied in a weak voice, "No, it's not mine. And no, I'm not alright! What about this makes you think that I'm alright?"

But the rudeness of her response was exactly what Gabriel was after. Not only did it get her talking, it also got her acting like her normal self again. Squeezing her hand while also giving her a smile, Gabriel calmly answered his sister, "I was only trying to get you back to yourself, and make sure that you weren't physically harmed."

Before Mary could offer a snide retort to her brother's words, their father cut in. "What happened Mary? If this isn't your blood, then whose is it? And why were you not asleep in your bed?" His father was clearly equally as angry as he was concerned for Mary at this moment, and would be until he figured out the entire story.

"But I was in bed, father. Or at least, I thought I was." This statement garnered confused looks from everyone. "I don't know how it happened, I must have walked in my sleep or something because I don't remember leaving my room after sundown last night."

"You're not wearing any sandals, and if your face and arms are anything to go by, your feet are probably just as blood soaked. Not to mention that dress isn't yours. Tell me the truth, Mary, or God as my witness, I'll take you to the courts to be tried for the crimes that have clearly been committed."

"Marcus!" their mother shrieked in outrage. "You will do no such thing. She's our daughter, not some common criminal. Let her explain how this came to be, and then we will decide what to do."

The four of them once again turned to Mary to see what she had to say. "As I was sleeping, I started to dream. I was in a field on the outskirts of town with a bunch of people and we were engaged in an orgy." This statement was met with gasps from everyone except Gabriel's brother, who clearly didn't understand the term. "It was just a dream!

There was no orgy! You wanted to know what happened and this is what happened, at least from my perspective," Mary defended.

"Very well," their father said through gritted teeth. "After your sinful dreams, what happened?"

"Well, I was in the middle of enjoying our neighbor Julius when suddenly I lost control of myself. I grabbed a rock and whacked him on the head as I went around and round to the others…ripping their hearts from their chests." It was here that Mary started to lose the life that had briefly returned to her eyes as she once again sought the refuge of their mother's arms.

"Well, apart from the Devil sending you dreams to tempt you further into sin, that doesn't explain how you came to be in this state," their father reiterated.

"When I woke up, I was in that field, surrounded by the thirty naked people with their hearts ripped out, dressed in this dress and covered in blood. And when I tried to scream, I had to claw my mouth open, there was so much blood. I don't know how I got there or how I managed to somehow see what was going on in my sleep. I'm scared father and I don't think I'll ever get the sight of that field out of my head."

From the look on her face, Gabriel believed his sister. While she was notorious for lying, he couldn't believe that she would lie about this. Lying about not having taken the last bit of pastry was a far cry from lying about how you came to be covered in blood.

Juba came back into the room then. "The tub is filled with water, Miss Mary. And I have left some incense burning to help you relax."

"Thank you, Juba," Mary said. "Mother, please, I don't want to be alone right now," she pled as she made her way to the other room.

"Of course, sweetheart," their mother said as the women left the dining room for the tub.

An uneasy silence followed as the men quietly contemplated what Mary had said. Gabriel believed his sister, but he could tell by his father's expression that he didn't accept the tale his daughter had told. Gabriel was about to try and convince his father of his sister's words, when his brother broke the silence. "What's an orgy?" he asked.

"Something that your sister should know better than to even mention in this house," their father answered. "It's a sinful congregation of the flesh that heathens engage in to praise their false gods. And that is the last of it that will be discussed by this family, is that understood?"

"Yes father," both boys said in unison. "But I hope that you can look past your hatred of sin, father, and see that Mary is telling the truth," Gabriel continued.

Upon hearing this, the patriarch rounded on his son. "What did you say?" he asked with an angry glare.

"I said I believe my sister, father. And I hope that you do as well. Mary may be many things, but she isn't capable of doing what she dreamed last night, physically or mentally. She may enjoy the sins of the flesh, but she's not a mindless killer." Gabriel hoped that his attempt to reason with his father was fruitful.

"Your love and compassion for your sister is admirable, Gabriel, but she is clearly in the thrall of the Devil. Her dreams alone are proof of that. And even you admit that she is a sinner. God in Heaven, even she admits it. How are we supposed to live when we have a servant of the Devil living in our own home? A servant of evil that has no control over her actions?"

"It may not be the Devil," Juba said, causing both Gabriel and his father to turn their heads to the family servant in search of an explanation. "Yesterday, when we were in the market, a man in long blue cloak came to me and said that the coven of witches that live outside of town had cursed the earth and this family."

"There's no such thing as curses, Juba," Gabriel's father declared. "And magic doesn't exist."

For the first time he could remember, Gabriel saw Juba disagree with his father. Shaking his head, he said, "Forgive me Master, but it does. Before I was brought to the Empire, the village I lived in had a woman with powers that no normal person could have. She mostly kept to herself, helping people recover from sickness and the like. But there was another woman who this woman was jealous of. She placed a curse on the woman, and soon that woman's husband was the husband of the woman with powers.

"You may not wish to hear it, Master, but magic is real. And the power the women at the edge of town possess is very real. Miss Mary may very well be under the curse that man spoke of."

Before his father could respond to Juba's words, Gabriel spoke up. "Juba's right father. While I'm reluctant to believe in curses, this same man came to me yesterday after we'd returned home. He said that the witches had cursed Marcus, and that the only way to end it was to kill the witches."

His father looked as though he was searching his mind for something; he paced around the table while he thought. "Marcus, come here." Upon these words, Gabriel felt a flicker of fear for his brother. Without meaning to, Gabriel had just sacrificed his brother in order to save his sister. As his younger brother approached their father, Gabriel had to swallow for fear of having his heart rise to his throat. Picking up his son, senior placed junior on the table. "Tell me the truth son, did anyone strange talk to you yesterday while we were in town?"

Marcus nodded his head. "Yes father, a woman came to me and asked if you were my father. And I told her that you were. She then asked me about Jesus, and why God would need to sacrifice His son for the world to believe in Him. So I explained to her that Jesus' death wasn't to inspire believe but to have original sin redeemed for all mankind; that all who believed in Jesus as the savior of man, and who lived good and just lives would be welcomed into Heaven." Gabriel was a little surprised by the articulation of his brother's answer, but he figured that it was around that age that he started to have a finer grasp of the world and his brother was following in his footsteps.

Gabriel felt a great sense of relief when his father also smiled at the boy's answer. "A very good and accurate answer. I'm actually quite proud that you were able to be so intellectual about our faith, son." Giving his son a hug, their father asked one final question as he looked at Juba. "And that was all you talked about; she didn't say or do anything else?" He released his son as he awaited the answer.

"No father," Marcus said as he shook his head. "Once I finished explaining it all to her, she seemed to summarize what I said in a sentence. That's when Juba arrived and I left to find you. I would've said something about this yesterday but she seemed nice and curious and I didn't want to cause trouble only because she made me have goosebumps."

"What do you mean she made you have goosebumps," Gabriel asked, positive he asked the same question his father was thinking.

"She scared me. Not like she snuck up behind me and said my name really loud, more like… I don't know how to describe it. There's something about her that makes me uncomfortable."

"She made you uneasy, you mean?" their father asked to clarify. When his brother nodded, Gabriel felt a sense of relief. It would appear that his brother hadn't been cursed. But that meant that Mary had become the servant of the Devil; he wasn't sure which was more upsetting. Turning to Juba, his father asked, "Does that line up with what she told you?"

"Yes, Master. I told her that, due to her lack of faith in Christ, that you would not be pleased to see her talking to your son. She said that she had simply asked him to explain your faith to her and that he had. That is when I took my leave of her and I found Marcus at your side," Juba said.

Heaving a sigh, Gabriel's father turned to him. "I don't know what this man who told you that your brother was cursed was trying to accomplish. But I want to hear no more of curses from any of you. I will go and see about what your sister claims to have dreamed into reality. You and your brother are to stay here and ensure that nobody comes or goes from this house while I'm gone. Do you understand?"

"Yes father," Gabriel said.

Nodding, his father took on a gentler tone than he'd had all morning. "Make sure your sister is alright. If she isn't responsible for everything she told us, I'll be back to ensure that she knows I love her and want her to recover." Gabriel nodded his understanding as his father turned back to Juba. "This man, the one that came to you and Gabriel, do you remember what he looked like." Juba just nodded. "Good, because after we investigate Mary's claims, we're going to find him and try to get some straight answers from him."

With that said, his father and Juba left the room and soon the house to get to the bottom of everything. Gabriel waited until he heard the door close before he turned to his brother. "Come on, we should see if Mary needs anything and tell mother what father has said." Together the two of them left the dining room and went to find their mother and sister.

Chapter 9
The Failure

After spending the night crying, Medea had no greater plan to explain her failing to her mother and grandmother. Both would be expecting her to reveal the identity of the man that would be the father to her daughter, to the next generation of their family's coven. But Medea had never been good at lying to them; whether through their power, or just being bad at the art of deception, her mother and grandmother could always tell when she was being dishonest with them.

But she had put this off long enough; it was nearly midday, and they would be waiting. Pushing herself away from the corpse of her father that she'd spent the past six hours clinging to in some vain attempt at self-comfort, Medea grabbed her dress. Walking over to where a patch of weeds was growing through the cobblestone floor of the temple, she gently unleashed her magic into the plant, causing it to grow. The weed wound itself first around her arms and then around her stomach as it cleared away all of her father's fluids that were still stuck to her.

Finally clean of the blood and semen from the previous night's spells, Medea put her dress back on. Walking over to her father's body one last time, she looked down upon him. "Forgive me father. It was never my intention to end your life so dispassionately. But the revelation of my upcoming failure broke my mind. I know that I will see you soon; mother and grandmother have never accepted my shortcomings and failures lightly. And to fail at such a moment as this…well let's just say that if you don't see me by the end of the day it will be a surprise to all of us. I hope that our time together in the underworld will make up for all the time we missed in life."

And without looking back, Medea focused on her home. She felt the silent impact on the air in her chest as thunder rumbled in the skies above. And the next thing she knew, she was staring at her home. The ancient and gnarled tree that her ancestors had hollowed out centuries ago, didn't look like it was the home of anyone. And it was for this reason that the coven was able to stay hidden and safe throughout the years as those fearful of their power sought to oust them from the community. But as she was about to enter, Medea had an idea about how to convince her family that she wasn't a failure.

Walking through the trunk of the tree that was spelled to act as a door, Medea found both her mother and grandmother waiting for her around the table. "By the rumble of thunder, I can see that you were at least half successful in your endeavors. But the real question is who is to be your mate?" her mother asked. For the first time in a very long time, there was a look of pride on her mother's face as she said all this.

But seeing the glimmer of motherly pride radiating from Circe, brought Medea's heart into her throat. *Not now! After all these years when I've yearned for it, why must you now show me that you are proud of me mother? Why is it my fate to constantly disappoint you; to be a failure?* Choking her doubts and heart down, Medea replied, "I'm not sure who he is, mother. I didn't recognize him." She forced herself to keep her expression impassive while she kept eye contact.

"Perhaps, you will meet him in the market the next time you are in town," her grandmother added in a hopeful tone. Then her tone and face darkened. "Or perhaps you will remember that you can't lie to me. Who is to father your daughter, Medea?" When she didn't immediately answer, her grandmother again demanded in her deadly calm voice, "Tell us who is to help you birth the next generation of our coven, Medea!"

And there it was, another idea, one that may help her achieve a greater victory over her mother and grandmother. "I don't wish to upset you. But since you insist on knowing; tell me how I'm supposed to bring about the next generation of our family's coven when we've already sentenced my daughter's father to death?"

"Speak plainly, Medea," her mother said with an irritated sigh. "Who is it?"

"The preacher's son; not the one you set the demon on, but the older one." Medea enjoyed the moment of stunned silence that her false revelation had brought. "Now, while the two of you try to figure out how to solve this problem that you've created, I'm going to take a bath. I can still feel my father all over me and I need to be rid of him once and for all. And I would like this moment of solitude to last." Throwing the led sickle that was still stained with her father's blood onto the table, Medea felt a rush like never before. She'd just lied to her family, gotten away with it and thrown a wrench into the scheme that had bothered her from its first conception, all while being able to tell off her family.

She would contemplate the dangers of being found out after her bath. The part about still feeling her father's fluids on her skin was true. She wasn't sure that the feeling of them being on her skin would ever go away. But at least the hot water and privacy would be a huge distraction and allow her to think about all that she had just put into motion.

Chapter 10
Juba

As he looked out upon the clearing, Juba's stomach gave a mighty lurch. Using all his willpower, he was able to keep his breakfast from rising up and adding to the horrid smells that came from the scene before him. But the smells were not the worst of it; that distinction was left for the eyes to witness. Bodies lay all over, naked with holes in their chests where their hearts had been ripped out. Hearts, he would soon discover that some had bites taken from them, lay as if haphazardly dropped.

But while the sight and smell of the massacre before him greatly upset Juba, it was the stillness in the clearing that most uneased him. There was no sound-no wind or animals to be seen. Given the sights before him, he would have thought that some crows, or maybe a pack of wolves would have been feasting on the bodies. But not even flies or maggots seemed to be feasting on the poor sinners.

Turning to his master, Juba said quietly. "We should not be here. Even the animals stay away; something is wrong here. Call it evil, call it magic, something unnatural happened here, Master, and we should not stay. At the very least, we must inform the town elders of what has happened here."

His master at first did not respond, as he gazed out upon the clearing. "Mary, what have you done?" he asked quietly to himself. Juba pretended not to hear this. But as Marcus made his way toward the center of the clearing, Juba hesitantly followed. "Some of this doesn't make sense, Juba. If someone was walking through an orgy ripping hearts out, you'd expect there to be one couple together, and everyone else scattered as they ran. But look, within the circle made from the torches, they're rings of sinners, all with their hands bloody, like they ripped their and their partners' hearts out themselves. Those that seemed to have run don't have bloody hands, meaning they didn't rip any hearts out. This makes no sense."

As Juba looked out at the bodies, he noticed the young couple that Mary had tried stealing from the day before, and his heart gave a small ache for the lives these sinners had. They didn't deserve this fate. "I agree, Master. But we will not discover anything more here. Darkness shrouds this clearing, and I do not wish to be caught up in it. Perhaps the man that tried to warn me and Master Gabriel about this will be able to provide some of the answers we seek."

As they made their way back to the town an uneasy silence fell over the pair. Finally, after about ten minutes his master finally turned back to him. "Tell me truthfully Juba, what has become of my daughter. I pray for her to turn away from sin every night and day, but this…this isn't Mary."

As Juba looked to his master, he saw his friend, who was always so sure of things and their place in God's plan, looking lost for the first time in all of his years of service.

Putting a hand on his shoulder, Juba said, "You are right Master, that is not Mary. Sadly, none of us can deny that she is a sinner; she lies, steals, disrespects authority, and enjoys pleasures of the flesh. She was clearly at that orgy, and she did not sleep walk there. But Miss Mary is not a killer; of that, I have no doubt. You have taught and disciplined her as much as you can, but she has as much will as both of her parents, and is in love with the thrills sinning gives her. And she has quite a talent for it. Mary may not be the proper daughter that we all want her to be, but she is smart and capable. After a certain point we have to stop praying for what we want and accept what we have. Your daughter is not going to stop enjoying sinning; or at least she would not have before this morning. You are always saying that God works in mysterious ways; perhaps this is Him answering your prayers, ridding the world of sinners and providing Mary with the greatest push to turn away from her sinful ways. Now, more than ever, we must show her the love of Christ, or lose her forever to the evils of the world."

"Thank you, Juba," his master said with a grateful smile. "Sometimes I forget how wise you are, and how well you know me. And if I ever forget to treat you as I should, please forgive me and trust that I do not do it intentionally. You're right, of course, Mary is a sinner through and through, and will not stop. This tragedy, or one just as traumatic, may be the only thing that can convince her to change her ways. But your advice to show her Christ's love now more than ever is what we should do. When we return home, please ensure that I hug my daughter and ensure that she is alright."

Hearing his friend's request, Juba simply nodded. They walked in silence the rest of the way to town. As they made their way to the center of town, they caught snippets of conversations discussing a dead body. Thinking someone had found the scene of the orgy massacre and reported it to the town's elders already, they asked the third person they heard discussing it about which dead body they spoke. They were surprised to hear not about the scene they'd just left, but of a single murdered man found in the old abandoned temple at the edge of town. Strangely, nobody seemed to know who the man was. Now slightly concerned that the man they sought was the victim, Juba and Marcus made their way toward the temple to see if the unknown dead man was the man they were looking for. This had the extra incentive of being where the elders would be.

There was a small crowd outside the temple, all apparently gathered to see and try to identify the man that had been found with his throat cut. Making their way into the temple, Juba and Marcus found themselves before the elders they'd sought. Looking to the corpse on the floor, Juba saw that he was indeed the man that had tried to warn him about the witches' curse.

But before he could inform his master of this fact, one of the elders spotted them and made his way over. The man appeared to be only slightly older than Marcus, but Juba knew that he was much older than he looked. Juba also didn't like him much, as he had an air of superiority bigger than the empire. "Ah, Marcus Iracundus, so strange to see you in a pagan temple; I had to do a double take to make sure my eyes weren't deceiving me."

"Yes, well, I came looking for the elders and was told that this is where they were. So, here I am, Elder Antonius." Juba could tell from his master's tone of voice that he didn't care much for the man either.

"Please don't tell me that you're filing paperwork to have your daughter disowned again. If she hasn't gotten her act together by now, she never will. And to be frank, the council is a little annoyed that you file the paperwork only to come back a week later to say that you've reconciled. This time will be the last we grant it, and we won't allow for you to undo it."

With most anyone, Marcus would have cut him off immediately, but since the council and elders could make life difficult for anyone on a whim, Juba knew he restrained himself. "I'll be sure to keep that in mind, but I'm not here about Mary. I wish to report a murder, several in fact." He paused to allow the elder to gasp at the news. The town rarely saw much crime, so to have so much murder happen in one night was unheard of. "About fifteen or twenty minutes outside of town to the northeast, you'll find a clearing with a ring of torches and about thirty bodies—"

"Thirty?" Antonius asked incredulously.

"They appear to have been engaged in an orgy, and were attacked before many could discover what was going on," Marcus continued as if he hadn't been interrupted.

"I-I'll send someone out there immediately. Northeast, you said?" Both Juba and Marcus nodded to the question.

"I suggest sending a few people. The scene is quite unsettling, not to mention that there's thirty or so bodies."

Antonius just nodded absentmindedly as he went to tell the other elders about what he'd just learned.

Turning back to Juba, Marcus nodded toward the body of the man lying on the ground. "Why do I have a feeling that that man is who we really came to town to see?" his master asked in a hushed tone.

"Because he is the man we came to question, Master." Juba responded just as quietly. "If I had to guess, I would assume that some combination of the witches came to ensure that he could not offer his help to us."

"Maybe…," his master mused as they left the temple. "But something seems wrong. If these women have the types of power that you suggest, surely they don't need something as mundane as a blade to kill someone? Based on the amount of blood, he died there, but there didn't seem to be any form of confrontation. Something's wrong with this scene." The two of them walked speedily toward the Iracundus homestead as they talked, trying to avoid everyone's attention.

"Perhaps, but this day has clearly been cursed. One of the things that that man said to me yesterday was that the very earth had been cursed. Perhaps we should try to warn everyone we can and try to leave town."

"We can't do that Juba. While we may not know how to fight this devilry, we must at least try. It would ruin all the progress I've made in this town, turning everyone slowly to the light of Christ, if we left at the first test of faith. As the Lord is our shepherd, I must be this town's shepherd. And like Christ, I will not abandon my flock in their time of greatest need."

Seeing the resolve and righteousness of his master's decision, Juba simply nodded. As they continued home, the pair walked in silence, steeling their souls to the fight ahead.

Chapter 11
Protector

For the past hour Gabriel had paced outside his sister's room, wondering how he could possibly let her know that nothing would stop him from protecting her. She'd spent nearly an hour with their mother washing away the blood that had so covered her this morning, but now she was alone in her room. Knocking on her door, Gabriel said quietly, "It's me. Can I come in?"

Fearing that his sister was going to ignore him, as she had for so long, Gabriel turned away from her room after a moment's silence. But when he heard the scrape of the door opening, he turned back with high hopes and surprise. There stood his sister, half hidden by the door, with a weak smile on her face and a haunted look in her eyes. "It's about time you knocked. I could feel and hear you pacing for the past hour." Stepping aside so he could enter, Mary continued, "I've been hoping that you would pluck up your courage so I wouldn't have to."

Confused by her words, Gabriel turned to her. Seeing her close the door, he was utterly flabbergasted when Mary threw her arms around him, hugging him tight to herself. Tentatively, Gabriel raised his arms and hugged her back, hearing her sigh as he did. "What do you mean that you were waiting for me?" he asked as he gently rubbed her back.

"I've forgotten how much I've missed this," she whispered, seemingly ignoring his question. Finally releasing her hold of him, Mary led him to the bed and sat the both of them down. "I mean exactly what I said, Gabriel: I wanted you to be the one to make the first move. If I had opened my door before you knocked, it would have been me selfishly demanding your help; and I didn't want to be selfish." Hearing that she didn't want to be selfish caused Gabriel to give her yet another confused look. "Besides, waiting for you to make the first move allows for you to feel like you're acting my hero. Imagine that, my little brother as my hero."

"Hey, I'm only twenty minutes younger than you!" Gabriel defended, instinctively bristling at the mention that she was technically older than him. "And I've been bigger than you since we were fifteen."

But if he had expected Mary to rebuke his claim, he was to be disappointed. Instead, she just gave a gentle laugh, and most bizarre of all, kissed his hand that he only now realized that she hadn't let go of. "True, you are bigger than me. All the more reason that you'd want to protect me. That's why I reached out to you when I walked in-you've been desperate for our bond since I severed it. It's only now that I've had it back that I can say how much I've missed it, missed you."

As she finished Mary once again put her arms around him and hugged him tight. "I wasn't even sure that you felt it," Gabriel whispered as he felt a tear roll down his cheek at her admission. The next few minutes were spent in silence as the two of them held each other tight. Finally unable to hold in his concern any longer, Gabriel gently but forcibly extricated himself from his sister's embrace. Lifting her chin so he could look into her eyes, he asked, "Are you alright, Mary?"

Seeming to know what breaking away from his gaze would imply to him, his sister held it for a long while as his question lingered between them. When he was about to ask her again, she took a deep breath as she turned away from him. It was when she curled herself into a ball, finally letting go of his hand, that Gabriel began to comprehend just how unpractical his question was. "No," she said in weak voice. "No, I'm not alright, Gabriel. Somehow, I am responsible for ripping the hearts out of my friends. One minute, I'm feeling my favorite sensation in the world; and the next, I watch in horror as my arms shove themselves into those around me and rip their hearts out. I-I… I even remember taking bites out of some and letting the blood inside spill out of my mouth, like some of my friends like me to do with their seed." Gabriel could have lived without the visuals that confession had stirred in his brain, but understood Mary's need for confession. "I can't stop hearing their screams, can't stop feeling and tasting their blood, can't stop seeing the fear and pain on their faces as my hands rip their hearts out. I just want it to stop, I need it to STOP!"

At her outburst, Gabriel flinched away slightly. But as she turned back to him and flung herself at his chest, he couldn't do anything but put his arms around her as protectively as he could. Feeling her shake and hearing her cry, as she clung to his chest, Gabriel gently rocked his sister, hoping the infantile motion and his gentle cooing in her ear would be enough to calm her, if only for the moment at hand. "Shh, shh. It's alright. That wasn't you, it was all a dream. It's all just a terrible dream."

Upon hearing his attempted words at comfort, Mary pushed herself away from him. Looking into his eyes, she wiped her own as a smile seemed to form on her lips. "You're so pure, Gabriel. You always have been, it's why you are father's favorite. But don't ruin this moment by matching that purity with gullibility. Please tell me that you didn't actually believe that dream lie I gave."

Surprised at her sudden change in behavior, Gabriel looked over his sister. "Yes, I believed you. But I shouldn't be surprised that you both knew about an orgy and were a participant in it. But why lie, Mary? That lie made father think that the Devil was sending you evil dreams and that you're in now in his thrall. Why risk all that, when the truth is much more believable?"

"Can you blame me for wanting, for just once in my life, to have you all not think the worst of me? That, while yes, I can engage in activities that make me little more than a whore, that I was wanting your love and kindness rather than scorn; which had I told the truth, would have certainly been what you all looked at me with in my time of need. I'm still in need, Gabriel. I reignited the bond between us to feel your primal love and need to protect me from the horrors of the world. Please, understand that I'm not in my right mind right now and that I need to be given the space and aid in returning to something that resembles normal." At the start of her defense, Mary had gotten off the bed and paced as she carried on. Now, as she finished, she knelt at his feet with his hands in hers as she pleaded for his help. "Please Gabriel, I need your help. In your arms I feel safe and calm, like your arms shield me from my memories. Please, just hold me with the love for your twin in your heart and mind."

Seeing the complete desperation in his sister's eyes, Gabriel had no choice but to lift her back onto the bed and envelop her into a hug as he felt his love for his sister flood from every physical connection they shared in that moment. Once again, he felt his sister sigh into the protection she felt in his arms. He was reminded of the fact that, like her, he had missed the connection that was innately between them since birth. It was like a part of him that had been missing for so long had finally been returned and he was whole again.

He lost track of the amount of time that he held Mary for. But both of them were nearly falling asleep when a gentle knock on the door startled them apart. Getting up from the bed, Gabriel and Mary made their way to the door; both seeming to understand that their private moment had come to an end as they opened the door to reveal their father.

All three seemed shocked to see the persons on the other side of the door. But it was their father that seemed to recover first. "Juba has prepared a late lunch, if you're hungry," he said, more to Gabriel than Mary.

Turning to look at his sister, to see if she was going to be alright, Gabriel saw her nod. "Go ahead, I'll be alright for now," she said with one final side hug.

Gabriel noticed his father's raised eyebrow at this as he returned the hug in kind. "You should get some food to; you haven't eaten since last night."

Mary nodded her agreement as she turned to their father. “I’ll join you in a moment. But I need to talk to father first.”

Nodding his understanding, Gabriel exited his sister’s room and made for the dining room. Turning back, he saw his sister step toward their father and embrace him as she had Gabriel when he first entered their room. The look of confusion was short lived on their father’s face as he returned the embrace in kind.

Chapter 12
The Infatuated

The bath had been just what Medea had needed. Her newfound strength had allowed her to keep the waters heated for over an hour as she scrubbed herself clean; cleaner than she could ever remember being. But while the warm waters mixed with her own herbal infusions had calmed her, now that she was out of them, her anxieties started to slowly return. Seated as she was, staring at herself in the mirror as she combed her hair, Medea reflected on her decision to lie to her mother and grandmother.

What surprised her the most was that they had believed her. Never in her life had both her mother and grandmother been fooled by her lies; her grandmother was most deft at sussing out the truth. The fact that she'd managed to hoodwink Hecate was a little disconcerting for Medea. She wondered if her mother and grandmother had spent the past hour trying to rationalize how the gods could allow such a catastrophe to occur: one of those who'd provoked their revenge was to father their next generation.

As she watched herself, Medea caught her cheeks flush as she briefly thought of the boy. She wouldn't deny that he was handsome. What surprised her about her own reaction to the thoughts of him was how not repulsed she was by the idea of him fathering her daughter. What would the girl look like, she asked herself. But before her mind could go any further, she forcibly stopped herself. She was getting ahead of herself; the demon had to be recalled and given a new purpose before she could even consider anything concerning the fake child she and the Iracundus boy would have.

Standing up, Medea grabbed the dress she had brought with her and put it on. Giving herself one final look in the mirror, Medea stilled her face and calmed her heart; it would do her no good to have them realize that she was lying now. Exiting the room that housed the washbasin, she descended to the main level of the home. Unsurprisingly, both her mother and grandmother were there, clearly awaiting her return.

Keeping her head high, Medea glided herself toward the table and sat down, switching eye contact between the two of them. How she wanted to be the one to break the silence, demanding to know if they'd formulated a plan to resolve the issues at hand. Instead, she anticipated their barrage of questions and accusations. She didn't have to wait long.

"Of all the stupid things you've done, this takes the crown. You couldn't find yourself a proper mate with magic; no, you had to go and chose the heir to the family we are trying to wipe from the world," her grandmother spat at her in the most annoyed toned. "By the gods, Medea, you are more hassle than you're worth."

"It wasn't my choice; the Fates weave our fortunes with little regard to our wishes. I don't like it any more than you do, grandmother, so stop accusing me of disappointing you.

Instead of insulting me, how about you find a way to resolve the issue at hand. My future daughter can't perform the rituals I performed last night if her father is killed by a demon shortly after her conception."

"You dare to give me orders, girl?" her grandmother fumed, raising from her chair.

Medea's fear didn't even have a chance to rise, as her shock was called forth by her mother's first words in this altercation. "She's right, mother." Her grandmother was clearly just as stunned as Medea was, judging by the look on her face; her mother always sided with Hecate when disparaging Medea. "Loath as I am to admit it, Medea has a point. Wasting our energies on berating her for something out of her control, while cathartic in this moment, won't actually accomplish anything. We need to figure out a way to solve this issue. Is there a way that you know of that would allow for the demon to not be removed from the task we've given him, while also ensuring that the boy lives?"

Her grandmother looked like she was about to explode in anger, Medea had never seen her this enraged. "No, of course, there is no way! You bound the demon to your will to kill those that worship the false god, and it will carry out that task until it's complete. To try and change that now would undo the spell and return the demon to the underworld; not to mention kill us all for invoking Trivia and Nemesis to aid in our quest. The goddesses of magic itself and revenge do not take lightly to the invoking of their names in spells that are abandoned! The demon must be allowed to kill the Iracundus family, or we will all die."

Heaving a sigh, Medea's mother looked at her with her familiar look of disappointment upon her face. "So, you are to be the death of me, daughter. As I have always feared and known."

"For all the times that I've wished to be rid of you, mother, it was never to be by my doing. I could never hurt you," Medea whispered sincerely.

Standing up, Medea made to leave but the looks she got from her mother and grandmother held her in place. "And just where do you think you're going?" her grandmother asked. "We haven't finished discussing your colossal failure and how we're to remedy it."

"You said that it couldn't be fixed. So, I'm going to try and convince the boy to impregnate me. Once he has, I'll kill him myself, saving the fluids so that when my daughter comes of age, she can attempt to perform the rituals she'll need to reach her full potential." When neither her mother nor grandmother offered further resistance to her plan, Medea walked out the door.

As she crossed the invisible barrier that protected her home from teleporting invaders, she concentrated on the Iracundus boy. And as thunder rolled overhead, she found herself walking down a street in town. Knowing that this was the street that her family's enemies lived, Medea chose a home at random and sat herself down on the lawn inside the stone wall that surrounded it. Heaving a deep breath, Medea began to laugh hysterically. But her hysterics soon turned to tears as she realized what she'd just done.

"Are you alright?" a voice asked from above causing Medea to stop crying in fear. Looking up, her stomach fell as she saw the person who'd asked about her wellbeing was the very person she wanted to avoid at all costs. It was the

Iracundus boy she'd lied to her mother and grandmother about seducing.

Trying to get herself up and away, Medea was held in place by the boy's gentle grip on her arm as he sat down beside her. "Hey, relax. You don't have to leave. Tell me what's bothering you, I might be able to help. If nothing else, it helps to let it all out to someone who's willing to listen; confession is good for the soul. My name's Gabriel."

His voice and face were so kind that the next thing Medea knew, she was introducing herself to him. "Medea-I'm Medea," she said with a slight shake to her voice. Why was she feeling so nervous? "And I'm fine," she continued as she wiped her eyes. "I just had a fight with my mother and grandmother, it's nothing new."

"Are you sure? Something must be bothering you if you've wondered so far to cry in some random stranger's yard about it. If it's nothing new, why are you here?" The genuine concern that Medea saw in his eyes was impossible to ignore, Gabriel was clearly concerned for her and her situation.

"I've never been able to lie to them, until today. But it's not that I lied to them, or even the fact that they've believed it," Medea confessed even as she wondered why she was revealing this at all. "It's the fact that even if I'd told the truth, they'd blame me and call me a failure. But when I told the lie, I threw a complication into their latest scheme. Since I'd been against it from the start, seeing them try to reconcile the two very differing positions that they'd need to take was almost worth the hassle of my deception."

"That sounds complicated. Do you want some advice?" he asked. Curious to see what he'd say, Medea nodded.

"Christ says that lying is wrong, and that the truth would always set the soul free. Not to mention, that by complicated the scheme your mother and grandmother were trying to enact, you've broken one of the Ten Commandments by dishonoring them."

Medea didn't think that this counted as advice, since he only seemed to be telling her that what she did was wrong. She was about to tell him this, but he continued. "But sometimes, we need to do the wrong things in order to do the right thing." When he saw her look of confusion at this, Gabriel elaborated. "For example, this scheme that your mother and grandmother had come up with, it can't have been all that noble."

"Why do you say that? You don't even know what it was," Medea accused.

"When was the last time you ever heard anyone use the term scheme in a noble context? The fact that you said scheme rather than say, plan, tells me that whatever it was, it couldn't have been just."

"What they planned was justified!" Medea defended. "I may think that they went a tad too far, but that doesn't mean that something didn't need to be done."

Raising his hands defensively, Gabriel said, "I'm sorry. I've clearly offended you; that was not my intention. Please forgive me, but I can only give my point of view with the information I've been given. All I meant by all this is that, sometimes the right thing is complicated, and that only by being true to yourself can you do the right thing.

"From what you've told me, you are not the same as your mother and grandmother. There's something fundamentally different between you and them that causes your constant fighting. All three of you need to find out what that difference is and come to terms with its existence if you are to ever have a healthy relationship in the future."

"Oh, there's no such thing as a healthy relationship in our family," Medea replied. "But that is some interesting advice: discover the source of our friction and come to terms with it." Smiling, she looked at the boy. Spotting the knife he kept at his hip and the scroll that he'd apparently brought outside with him, Medea tried to assemble an understanding of Gabriel. "And what about yourself, Gabriel? How does the man who quotes Christ when giving advice to a stranger also be an avid reader of poetry with godly characters whose existence in the narrative defies the religion that he so believes?" she asked indicating the scroll at his side.

"I swear you'd get along with my father, talking like that. But no, the presence of the Olympians in the Iliad doesn't make it instantly blasphemous-at least not to me. The way I see it, Zeus, Ares, Aphrodite and all the others, could just be names for angels that the Greeks came up with, or different angels entirely. If each person has a guardian angel, there must be millions in Heaven; we can't know all the names for every single angel."

"That's an interesting compromise. But what about your father; does he share this angel theory?" Medea wasn't sure which answer she'd thought would be the better one for the boy to say his father ascribed to.

"With regards to me, he lets it slide because he knows that I don't pray to the Olympians as gods, or angels for that matter. I pray to God the Father and His son Jesus Christ. Should I pray to the angels, it's always done in generic ground terms, like 'angels watch over my sister'. But if other people were to start saying similar things about the Olympians and how they could really just be angels, my father would not be happy. He believes that the gods that once held dominion over these people are false gods at best and mouth pieces for the Devil at worst." The boy clearly thought that this practice was slightly wrong, but would never say that to his father; probably in fear of breaking the Commandment he described earlier.

"Well," Medea replied, "It seems your way of thinking would better allow for more religions to be subsumed into the faith of Christ; shame your father doesn't realize that." Medea turned herself to fully look upon Gabriel. As she gazed at him, his black hair, his brown eyes, she realized that he wasn't really a boy, but a man. It was then that she remembered why she was here, and her face flushed as the images came to her.

But before Gabriel could take notice of her flush, a girl who was clearly his sister came out of the house. "Oh, there you are! I've been looking all over for you!" she exclaimed as she walked over toward them.

Realizing that she wouldn't get a chance to properly seduce the young Iracundus, Medea stood to leave. "Right, I should be going," she said, but was overpowered by Gabriel, as he too stood up upon his sister's arrival.

"Mary, I'm sorry to keep you, but Medea and I were just having a great conversation." It was only after he had introduced her that Mary looked to Medea with what she would have sworn was jealousy bathing in the girl's eyes. "Why don't you and Juba bring the rest of lunch out here and the three of us can have it together?"

“Alright…,” Mary said slightly crestfallen. She turned back the way she came and returned inside.

“I hope that wasn’t you inviting me to eat. Forgive me, but I must be on my way.”

“Are you sure?” he asked, seemingly hurt that she wouldn’t be staying. “I was just starting to get into our conversation.”

“No, I really must be going. I should go try and figure out why I’m always fighting with my mother and grandmother.” Gabriel nodded and wished her luck. As he turned to the sound of commotion coming from the entryway, Medea took her chance. Whispering quietly as she could, Medea wove a quick but effective protection spell around him, “*Protection, full and unyielding, I place upon you!*” It was as he turned back to her that she placed the kiss that sealed her protection of him on his cheek.

Before he could question what was happening, she was gone. Running through the front gate and down the street, Medea could hear him giving lazy chase. Looking down an alleyway, she noticed it was empty. Turning down it, Medea let thoughts of home carry her feet, as thunder rolled overhead.

Chapter 13
The Reluctant Spy

After Medea's strange, abrupt departure that afternoon, Gabriel had spent the remainder of the day by his sister's side. Mary had seemed unwilling to leave him be until shortly after dinner. Giving her a brief one-armed hug and a kiss to the top of her head, Gabriel told his sister that he was going to retire to his room for the rest of the night.

"Ok, good night," she replied with a slightly sad look in her eyes. "I think I'm going to stay up a bit later and spend some time with mother." And with a slightly happier face, she made her way to the dining room where her mother was sitting.

Gabriel started making his way back to his room, but only got about halfway before he remembered that he'd left his scroll in the dining room. Turning back, Gabriel quietly walked in the wake of his sister as he didn't want to interrupt the conversation her and their mother were undoubtedly engaged in. "…issed Gabriel's cheek and then just ran off. It was weird; there was this look in her eyes, almost like she was judging him," he heard his sister say, stopping him in his tracks.

Staying behind the wall, Gabriel continued to eavesdrop. "Well, it's nice to see that you're finally starting to care for your brother," he heard his mother say.

"I've always cared for Gabriel!" his sister immediately defended. "I've searched this entire town, looking for someone worthy to be his wife for the past five years. I know every girl our age, but that girl's face was unfamiliar to me. He said that she said she lived in town, but if she does, something is wrong. What if she's one of the witches that cursed us?"

It appeared that both Gabriel and his mother were stunned by this revelation and line of inquiry. Could his sister's sinful nature have actually been her trying to find him someone worthy of marriage, at least in her eyes? And Gabriel had never considered that Medea was one of the witches that had apparently cursed their family. Although, the name Medea was a fairly famous witch from the stories of Jason and the Argonauts.

"Well, that's certainly a revelation," his mother said, finally recovering. "But if she's one of the witches, why would she be judging your brother as you seem to think she was doing? Why would she kiss him?" she asked, voicing the thoughts Gabriel had also had. "But ignoring that all for a moment, let me ask: in your five-year search for your brother's bride, did you ever find anyone that was suitable? What would you have even deemed appropriate, out of curiosity?"

"Someone who wouldn't fall prey to my seductions, someone who claimed to be saving themselves for marriage. And of course, I didn't find anyone! Do you think

I would search this small town for five years if I had found someone? I'm irresistible, just like my mother."

"And what is that supposed to mean?" Gabriel could hear the angry edge in his mother's voice and could just imagine the look she'd be giving Mary.

"It simply means that you are beautiful mother. Half of the men I've been with wanted me to pretend to be you. You inspire so much lust in this town, I'm surprised father hasn't forced you to stay inside at all times."

"I'm not sure if I should take that as a compliment or an insult," his mother said, sounding truly unsure. "But I do know that I never want to hear you say that again. And *never* tell your father. Small as it is, I do enjoy my freedom." There was a moment's silence, as the two seemed to share a moment's understanding, and Gabriel wondered if he should forget about the scroll and just return to his room and try to forget what he'd heard. But then his mother spoke again, and he continued to listen in. "But let's return to the point about this girl that spiked your jealousy."

"Jealousy?" His sister sounded offended by the notion. "I was not jealous. I—"

"There was a girl sitting alone with the boy you were expecting to spend the afternoon with, who kissed him when she left. You said yourself that you've missed the closeness that you and your brother share now that you've opened up to him again-whatever that means. This girl was, in your eyes, encroaching on the attention that Gabriel should have been giving you. Face the facts, Mary: she made you jealous." His mother's voice was gentle as she explained this to her daughter.

"It's not a sin to be protective of my brother," Mary quietly rationalized, but Gabriel could hear that she's accepted the fact that she'd gotten jealous of Medea in her voice.

"No, it's not," their mother quietly reassured. "But why do you feel so uneasy about her. From what Gabriel said at dinner, she was simply looking for a place to quietly think things over away from her problems. What about that raises your suspicions?"

There was a long pause as Gabriel could feel his sister struggle with how to express her feelings. Finally heaving a frustrated sigh, Mary said, "I don't know." Gabriel heard the scrape of a chair, followed by his sister's pacing as she tried to find the words. "I spied on them for a moment before I announced myself. She barely looked at him until just before I did, and when she did, she got this look. It was like she was about to do something, but my arrival stopped her. And then as me and Juba were bringing things out for lunch, right before she kissed him, she whispered something while doing this motion with her hands, like she was tightly wrapping a piece of cloth around itself. Add that to the fact that I don't recognize her, and I cannot think of another explanation other than she's one of the witches from the outskirts of town."

"Have you talked to Gabriel about this? You say that you can feel one another and sense each other's emotions. Surely, he sensed your unease about the girl."

"He might have if I let him," his sister said, as he heard her flop back into a chair. "As soon as I felt and… *saw* his attraction for her, I welled up my feelings somewhere he wouldn't feel them."

"Ok, I can't pretend to understand what you're talking about," his mother said in exasperation. "Can you please explain this supposed connection between you and your brother."

"What do you mean you don't understand? I'm saying exactly what I mean. As twins, me and Gabriel, I don't know, have this instinctual bond that allows us to communicate with each other in a way that most people can't. And it's not just us, the Ovapasch twins, Kara and Nikki, feel it too." Mary paused as she seemed to judge their mother's understanding. Clearly, she was still confused as Mary continued, "Ok, you know how you can just look at me or Gabriel or Marcus and know something is bothering us or we've done something we shouldn't have or we just need a hug." Although he couldn't see her do it, it was clear from his sister's next words that their mother had nodded to this. "Well, it's like that, but maybe a little deeper. We just have this understanding of each other."

"And you've purposefully closed off this connection between the two of you for the past decade, only opening it this morning?" Again, he couldn't see it from behind the wall, but Gabriel assumed that his sister nodded at his mother's question. "Why?"

"When I found myself in that field, covered in so much blood, I was terrified. More terrified than I've ever been in my life. I saw my friends lying on the ground, their hearts ripped out, and their blood on my hands, and I needed to feel safe. Gabriel, as much as I've ignored and annoyed him for the last ten years, is the person who I know would never hurt me, deny me or let me down. When I came home this morning, I wanted nothing more than for my brother to hold me and tell me that nothing would ever hurt me again. So, I opened myself to him, as he's wanted me to do ever since I shut him out. But in doing so, I also saw myself in his eyes, and how I ruined our relationship by closing up in the first place. That's why I tried to spend so much time with him today: to try and make up for the way I've treated him." As Mary said all this, Gabriel could feel the sadness and regret that rolled off her from the other room so strongly that he was knocked back a step and tears were starting to fall down his face in rivers.

As he tried to hold back his sobs, his sister clearly was not. He heard her crying as his mother got up and went to her, cooing gentle reassurances. Seeming to calm down, but still clearly feeling upset, Mary drove an emotional knife in Gabriel's heart. "That's not the worst of it. When he said goodnight to me just a few minutes ago, he was annoyed that I had wanted to spend more time with him. I don't even think he realized that he felt it, it was so fleeting; but the fact that he was annoyed by me seeking the comfort his mere presence brings me, it hurts. But I can't say that I blame him, we've grown apart over the years; maybe he's just gotten used to the idea that I'd never let him back in and this change was too drastic to happen all at once."

"Oh, sweetheart, I'm sure that if you tell your brother this, he'd apologize for upsetting you. You said yourself, he would never hurt or deny you."

How Gabriel wanted to just go into the dining room and give his sister a hug, and tell her he was sorry for hurting her. The pain he felt coming from the room was starting to become unbearable. Feeling that if he stayed another moment, he'd get himself in trouble by revealing that he was listening in secret, Gabriel turned to return to his room. Resolving to spend the foreseeable future with Mary as much as she wanted, Gabriel took a single step back toward his bedroom. "Take one more step, Gabriel, and I'll never forgive you!" he heard his sister call out, stopping him in place.

Knowing that she meant it, Gabriel turned back to the dining room and walked into the doorway. Seeing the shock on his mother's face was only a fleeting observation as his eyes found his sister's. "Please don't shut me out again," he pleaded to her in a whisper.

She didn't respond at first, just got up and walked over to him. Staring into each other's eyes, Gabriel let his regret at hurting her flow like Vesuvius on Pompeii. After what seemed like an eternity to him, Mary threw her arms around his torso, clinging herself tightly to him, as she'd done early that day in her room. "I'm sorry for shaming you, but I really needed this," she said as fresh tears began to fall down her face and onto his chest. Gabriel just kissed her head and rocked them gently from side to side.

Seeing his mother stand from her chair brought Gabriel back to the present and broke the spell the moment he and his sister were sharing had created. "How long were you listening?" she asked him with a slightly angry look.

"The whole time," both he and Mary said together.

The shock of hearing them talk in unison seemed to dissipate whatever anger their mother was feeling. "It's been a long time since you two did that. There really is a connection between you, isn't there?" Gabriel just nodded, feeling Mary do the same against his chest. "Well then, I think I'm going to head to bed. Goodnight children."

Walking over to the pair of them, their mother gave them both a kiss before enveloping them both into a hug. "Mind your sister, Gabriel; she needs you tonight." Nodding, Gabriel unwrapped an arm from between the three of them to return his mother's hug. Releasing them, their mother left the dining room.

And then it was just him and Mary.

Finally releasing him, Mary interwove her hand into his as she led them to her bedroom. "You'll stay with me all night, right?" she asked with a desperate look once they were in her bedroom.

Nodding, Gabriel crawled into the bed with her. "What kind of brother would I be if, after all that, I just left in the middle of the night?"

"The worst kind," she said as she snuggled closer to him. For a while, Gabriel just held Mary gently to himself, thinking that she would fall asleep in his arms. "You can ask me," she said quietly into his chest, startling him from his quiet reflections.

"How come you can read me so much better than I can read you?" That wasn't what he'd been thinking about, but with her just telling him to ask, it came to the forefront of his mind. "I barely feel a thing from you, but it's like you know what I'm thinking the moment I think it."

Pulling herself away from his chest so she could look him in the eyes, Mary gave him a weak, sad smile. "Because I'm still holding things back from you. Not because I don't love and trust you, but because I'm scared and hurting on the inside and I don't want you to have to feel that way. It's all I can do to not cry and curl up in a ball for the rest of my life." Taking his hand, Mary placed it over her breast, where he could feel her heart beating steadily. "If you weren't here, my heart would be beating faster than a pack of wild horses. You're keeping me together, Gabriel, and I don't want you to feel the things that are tearing me apart. I know that it's cruel to abuse our connection like this, but right now, I need to be selfish in order to get back some sense of normalcy. I'm sorry that that means that you can't read me as well as I can read you, brother, but please believe that I wish that this wasn't the case. We used to be able to have entire conversations with barely any words, and I would like to experience that again one day."

"You're doing too much for my sake, Mary," he said, meaning more than just sparing him her emotional pain "I can cope." There was a long moment where the two siblings just looked into each other's eyes. When she closed her eyes, Gabriel could feel it, the pain, confusion, fear; the fear caused the hairs on the back of his neck to stand on end and his heart to beat at an unnaturally fast pace. It was only after he'd pulled her close to him that he began to feel himself calm down. Breathing heavily as if he'd just run around the town five times, Gabriel tried to pull the negative emotions swirling around in his sister into himself, wanting to remove whatever of her burden that he could.

It was the first time that he felt himself affecting their bond since it had been re-established. The more he took upon himself, the more he felt Mary relax in his embrace. He'd took upon most of her pain and fear into himself when he felt a jab of resistance. "Don't take it all, Gabriel. Thank you, a million times thank you, you selfless fool; but I will not let you be burdened by my sins, hero or not. Besides, if you take it all, we're just going to have the same problem.

You've taken the worst of it, that is enough for both of our needs."

Feeling his heartbeat increase before levelling out, still at a higher than normal pace, Gabriel pulled Mary tight to himself before whispering a final goodnight in her ear. It wasn't long after that that both were asleep in the arms of the other.

Chapter 14
Juba

As he went about preparing breakfast for his master and his family, Juba noticed that both Gabriel and Mary were sitting at the dining room table. Taking the meat he'd been cooking off the stove, Juba went to join them for a moment. He was still concerned for Mary, and wanted to ensure that she was feeling better this morning. "Good morning, you two. You are certainly awake earlier than usual," he greeted his young masters.

"Good morning, Juba!" the two of them said in unison. This, along with their easy smiles gave Juba pause. He could barely remember the two of them being so at ease with each other since their brother was born.

And then he saw that they were holding hands. "Do my eyes deceive me, or are you two actually getting along? Or is this a continuation of yesterday's comfort seeking?"

Turning towards him, Mary responded, "It's both. Last night we finally got everything cleared out between us. We're back to about where we were ten years ago, when I shut Gabriel out."

The way she said that confused Juba. "'Shut Gabriel out'?" he asked the twins.

"It's not important," Gabriel answered. "It's a twin thing, you wouldn't understand."

Juba just nodded to this. "Well, regardless of its importance, I am happy to see the two of you close once again," he said as he returned to cooking breakfast. To ensure the food was served warm, the preparation area was right next to the dining room, which allowed Juba to hear the conversation that Gabriel and Mary engaged in.

"Speaking of things not understood," Gabriel began.

"Oh, you're finally asking," his sister answered, seeming to know what he was talking about.

"I am," Gabriel said with a nod of his head. "It wasn't all for me, was it?"

"Good Lord no," Mary responded, shaking her head emphatically. "I enjoy being a seductress too much for you to be the only reason for my fornications. I didn't even realize that it was something I was doing until recently. The girl was being annoyingly stubborn which brought out a strange reaction in me. I was both annoyed and giddy at the same time, which led me to question why I felt giddy. I actually left Alexandria to figure out this confluence of emotions."

"Wait! Alexandria as in the daughter of Elder Antonius, that Alexandria?" the boy questioned his sister.

Intrigued by this potential revelation, Juba looked up from the bread he was cutting and watched the response Mary gave. All she did was smile at Gabriel. "Is that jealousy that you're feeling brother? What could you possibly have to be jealous of? Surely, it's not that your whore of a sister seduced the pagan's daughter before you got a chance to even introduce yourself to her properly?"

There was a glimmer of mischief in the girl's expression as she seemed to toy with her twin. "Why would such a firm believer in Christ be so keen as to wonder at the virginal status of a pagan, who his faith denounces and denies his wish to wed?"

"I never said I wanted to marry her!" Gabriel rebuked his sister, but that was clearly the wrong thing to do, as Mary's smile just grew. Bowing his head, Gabriel said, "Fine, I could think of worse fates than to be married to Alexandria; she's quite beautiful and, if her father's boasting is to be believed, intelligent. Differences in faith aside, I don't think it would be a bad match. Clearly you think so too, if it was her that made you realize that you've been secretly searching for my bride all these years."

This stunned Juba, but it was clearly what the two of them were talking about. Apparently, last night really had laid all their secrets bare. But before Mary could respond, the rest of the family entered the dining room. His master had made a bit of fuss over the fact that Mary not only joined them for breakfast, but had beaten him to the table. She blamed it on Gabriel no longer snoring as he guarded her to ensure that she didn't sleepwalk again last night.

After breakfast, Marcus had returned to town to see what the council had learned about the murders that had taken place the night before last. Bathsheba had left shortly after her husband to go see their neighbor Julius Captus in her ongoing attempt to help him overcome the death of his late wife. Juba, as always, obeyed his master's orders and kept an eye on Mary stealthily. To do this, he asked her for her assistance in making the dress he had planned on making for her parents with the material that he'd acquired from Meredith a couple of days ago.

When Mary had come to his assistance, Gabriel's hand in hers, she got an eager look on her face. "And just who is this dress for, Juba?" she asked with a mischievous smirk. "Both my and mother's birthdays have passed; could it be that you've found yourself a lady love at last?"

Remembering the particularly vigorous lovemaking that had been a part of the purchase of this fabric, caused Juba to blush upon hearing his young mistress' insinuation. "No, I am making this for your mother," he explained. "Your father is particularly fond of this color, and I thought a beautiful dress in your father's favorite color would be an excellent anniversary gift." Juba was pleased to see the surprise on both of the twins' faces as he revealed this. But then he thought he saw something darken Mary's features, but as soon as it came, it was gone.

"So, what do you need my help with?" Mary asked. "You know mother's measurements as well as she does. And as much as I'd like to be built like her, sadly I'm not," Mary remarked with a sad look toward her chest. Both Juba and Gabriel briefly followed her line of sight, before turning away with a blush.

"You are right," Juba agreed, unable to look her in the eye. "But it is not your silhouette that I am after, it is your mind." Seeing the confusion on Mary's face in the periphery of his vision, Juba forced himself to look back into her eyes, despite the heat he could feel in his cheeks. "You are an expert in the art of seduction, if you will permit me to say so. And I was hoping that you would offer your expertise in these matters when it came to the style of the dress."

Mary's glee was written all over her face as Juba elaborated his need for her. Juba thought she was going to start jumping for joy, but then she reined herself in as she turned to her brother. "You know Gabriel, I do believe Juba just asked me to seduce my own father," she said in a serious tone, one that now matched her face.

"And you love the naughtiness of that idea," Gabriel responded with a smile on his face. Juba didn't know all the details of what had happened between them yesterday, but something clearly had. It had been nearly a decade since the two of them had spent this much time together without one or both of them complaining about that fact; and the fact that Gabriel had just encouraged her sinful nature was a sign that a dramatic change in their relationship had occurred.

"Oh God in Heaven, yes!" Mary squealed. Clasping her hands together in front of herself, she gaily jumped over to Juba's side. "You have no idea how long I've waited for this sort of opportunity, Juba," she said as she threw her arms around him. "To seduce father has long been my secret ambition. I can't count the nights that I've spent thinking of the ways that I could achieve this level of sinful pleasure," Mary revealed as she turned to look at the cloth intently. Juba was slightly surprised that both Mary revealed such a sinful wish, and that Gabriel didn't do anything to reproach her for having such thoughts toward their father.

Running her hands over the green material, Mary's gleeful smile became serious. Turning to Juba, she said, "If you are serious about wanting me to help design this dress, Juba, I need you to promise that you will never reveal to my parents that I helped. If either of them knew what I'm about to reveal, they'd final go through with disowning me and despite our constant fighting, I don't want to be kicked out of this family," she said as she looked back to Gabriel. Her twin just nodded as he came to join them, once again taking Mary's hand into his own.

"I understand Mary, should they ask, I will tell them that I bought the dress as is in the market," Juba swore to his young mistress solemnly. "You will not be mentioned."

Seeing his sincerity in his eyes, Mary nodded. "Thank you, Juba. Despite everything, you've always been kind to me and let me indulge in my pleasures, and I've always been grateful for that." With the hand that wasn't holding her brother's, Mary took his and kissed it. "Usually, a true and proper seduction would take a few months of work and reconnaissance to see what the mark likes and how to best utilize your assets to enthrall them. But, seeing as I've already done this, we can move ahead to making the dress to accentuate mother's assets to full effect. But it is there that we run into a small but crucial hiccup." She turned to Juba and Gabriel as if she hoped that one of them would reveal what hiccup she was alluding to. Giving a small sigh of exasperation, she continued, "Mother and father have been married for many years and have had sex numerous times. By this time in their marriage, things have become routine. This dress needs to break them out of that routine thinking. Thankfully, I know just how to do that, while also keeping it seductive."

"And how do you plan on doing that?" asked Gabriel, engaging in the dress making for the first time.

"What was the first thing that you noticed about the girl from yesterday? We both know that you found her attractive, but what about her drew you to find her so? Or Alexandria, why are you attracted to her?" Mary asked her brother as a form of response to his question.

Juba didn't understand where exactly this line of questioning was supposed to lead, and it seemed that Gabriel didn't either. But that didn't stop his young master from blushing at the questions his twin was asking him. "Their faces, I find that both Medea and Alexandria have pretty faces. But what I'm most attracted to in both of them is their intelligence; I don't know either of them very well- I think I've spent five hours with the two of them combined- but they, I don't know, exude this intelligence. That's what really attracts me to them, how they give off this aura of intelligence," the boy said as he seemed unable to fully look at his sister.

"And that is why the past five years have been so difficult for me, brother dear," the girl said as she tapped his chest lightly with her free hand that wasn't busy holding his. "Because unlike the majority of the male population, you are not simply satisfied with a set of naked tits and holes to stick your penis in. Thankfully, for the purposes of this dress, we are dealing with someone much less complicated. And while father has his own kinks that make him more challenging than most, he is child's play in comparison to you."

Mary was once again staring at the green material laying before the three of them. Reverently running her hand over it, she continued, "Where most men look at mother and lust after her breasts, father's focus is more often drawn a little lower. Don't ask me how I know this, but while I know that he enjoys playing with mother's boobs, it's her ass that our father truly lusts after. I don't know if mother actually knows this as she thinks her boobs are enough to please; they are her pride and joy for staying so lofty even after three kids. That's the key to a good seduction: knowing what you've got and what your partner likes and weaponizing that knowledge to the fullest potential." Turning to look fully at Juba, Mary's eyes sought out those of the family's trusted servant. Once their eyes were locked, she spoke in the most serious tone Juba had ever heard her use. "If you want this to succeed to its fullest potential, Juba, you will need to accomplish three things that will be nearly impossible to do so. First, you must make a dress that both showcases and hides my mother's breasts and bottom; each must be displayed enough to entice the gaze of my parents, while also keeping the other's eyes from noticing the extent to which they are displayed. Second, you mustn't allow them-at least for this first use-to know that you are the one giving the dress; they are more likely to feel amorous if they think the dress was a gift to them from the other. Lastly, you will need to relay to me, in as graphic detail as you can, every word and action they take on their anniversary so that I may enjoy the fruits of the greatest seduction in my life."

Juba wasn't sure that he could fulfill the requirements that his young mistress seemed to deem essential to the success of his simple gift idea. "Mary, what you ask is very inappropriate. You have clearly put a lot of thought into this over the years, and I thank you for the advice that you've given me. I will try my hardest to put it to the best use that I can. But to divulge to you the secrets of your parents' love, to spy on them on the day of their blessed union, is a betrayal of trust that I cannot commit against your father and mother. I will respect your wish to leave you out when I tell them that I am the one who is giving the dress, but I would like you to respect my wish that you do not ask me to betray their trust in such a way, and that you do not spy on them yourself for your own sinful pleasure. Your parents are devout followers of Christ, and their marriage bed should not be soiled in such a sinful matter on such a special and holy occasion."

Juba saw the fire of rebellion in Mary's eyes at his request that she act in a manner her parents would approve of for one day, and he feared that she would fight him on this point. But that fire died the moment Gabriel released her hand and brought his to her shoulder. Both Mary and Juba turned to the boy as he said, "Thank you Juba, that is an acceptable arrangement. You can even say that it is a further gift from Mary and myself, as I will ensure that she doesn't go back on her word." Mary opened her mouth as if to refute her brother's claims, but he shook his head. "No, sister. Besides the fact that Juba is right, you owe it to mother and father to be a daughter they are proud of, if only for one day. You get to live out your fantasy, regardless; and your imagination is much more potent than whatever reality unfolds."

There was an uneasy silence that followed Gabriel's words. Juba wondered if Mary would storm off in protest to all her brother and him were saying. But as he watched the twins, Juba was struck by something; he couldn't put his finger on what made him think it, but he would have sworn that the two of them were having a conversation entirely without words. Mary smiled an amused smile as Gabriel blushed while boldly looking into his twin's eyes. With a defeated sigh, Mary turned back to Juba as she took her brother's hand once again into her own. "Very well, Juba, you have my word. I swear that I will not try and spy on my parents on their anniversary, and that I will simply allow my imagination to fill in the gaps of my greatest seduction. As my brother said, he will ensure that I am the demure daughter that they've always wanted me to be, on that day to make them proud." Turning to leave the room, she took a few steps toward the bedrooms with her brother in tow before turning back to Juba. "While I'm not proportioned like my mother, I do have a dress that does showcase my bottom in such a way as I've described. I'll model it for you to see how the design works later tonight." And before Juba could respond, the two of them were gone, retreated to one of their bedrooms.

Chapter 15
The Secret Admirer

Rather than going to her room, which had seemed like her sanctuary for the past day and a half, Gabriel was surprised to have his sister lead them into his room. Pulling the door open, Mary let go of his hand as he made his way to his bed and she closed the door behind them. Ever since the previous night when he'd taken the majority of her emotional pain into himself, Gabriel had finally been able to read his sister as easily as she had seemed to read him for all of yesterday; and he used that ability to gauge her feelings about what had just happened. But either he wasn't as skilled as she was at this or his sister was confused, as her thoughts and feelings seemed to be aswirl and nothing seemed to be sticking to the surface of her tumultuous mind. But as she came back to him, snuggling her back to his chest, everything calmed and she became calm and content. "How is it that you can stand that sea of confusion?" he asked to the back of her head.

He felt her laughing against him before she turned herself to face him. Looking into her eyes, Gabriel felt the love his twin had for him lazily roll off Mary and envelop the two of them. "For someone so attracted to intelligence, you don't always have the greatest grasp on it," Mary said playfully. "Even after last night, even after you took my pain and anxiety, I'm still scared. You felt it and because it didn't belong to you, you were able to let it go. I'm not so lucky.

"Please understand Gabriel, I ripped the hearts out of my friends, felt their blood flow down my fingers and chin, and I couldn't stop myself. And to find out that three witches at the edge of town cursed our family was the reasoning why; it's not an exaggeration to say that the past couple of days has been a lot to take in." Despite her composure, and how she felt safe in his arms, Gabriel felt the turmoil in his sister rise once again. "What you did last night made me functional, but it will be a long time before I'm back to my old self."

Pulling her in tighter to himself, Gabriel offered the only support he could give. "Tell me what I can do to help."

"You already are," she said into his chest. For a while Gabriel thought that Mary was falling asleep, but then she pushed herself away slightly from him. "I want you to distract me, brother dear. Like how you thought that naughty, dirty thought to convince me to agree to your ridiculous stipulation that I don't enjoy the fruits of my years of labor."

Gabriel blushed as he recalled the image of his parents in a most intimate embrace that he'd imagined not ten minutes before; and to his horror, he felt his groin tense up as he flashed himself in place of his father. Trying with all his might to erase that image from his mind, Gabriel knew better than to look at his sister. She could probably see the thoughts that were holding his mind captive; had he taken more than just her pain last night?

“My, my, what is that deliciousness in your mind, Gabriel?” Mary asked, causing him to look his twin in the eyes, despite his knowing better. The smirk his sister was giving him was full of the mischievous sexuality that had been present in her for the past five years. Even without her words, that smirk was enough to inform him that he really needed to learn how to keep her from his mind. But it was when she looked down between them that Gabriel really felt the depths of his embarrassment. “And what is THAT?” Mary asked with positive glee.

“Hey!” Gabriel shouted in an unnaturally high-pitched voice when he felt Mary’s hand around his penis. He tried to pull himself away, but her grip was tight as she deftly and quickly took stock of his size.

When she finally released him, Mary had a most satisfied smile curling the edge of her lips. “I think I’ve lost the right to call you my little brother, well and truly now.” Gabriel couldn’t help the swelling of his ego at that moment. If such an expert in such matters as his sister said it, he couldn’t deny the truth. “I was really hoping that you were more like father, but I guess that you’re more like mom than I am.” A look of slight disappointed annoyance came upon Mary’s face as she said this last truth.

“Can we not talk about our parents and sex please; it makes me uncomfortable,” Gabriel said, hoping that she’d allow the change in topic.

“Very well,” Mary replied after a moment’s pause. “Why don’t we talk about your crush on Alexandria instead?”

"It's not a crush!" Gabriel tried to defend himself, something that he seemed to be doing a lot of lately. "You're the one that suggested she be my bride. Why do you think such a thing in the first place?"

"You mean what about her made me realize that I'd been searching for a girl to be your bride all these years?" Mary reiterated his question, to which he just nodded. Turning onto her back and looking to the ceiling, Gabriel could almost see the wheels turning in his twin's head as she tried to find the words to answer his question. "She said no," Mary finally revealed as she turned her head to look at him.

"I thought you were irresistible, that nobody had refused you," Gabriel teased. "Or were you lying to mother last night and simply bragging?"

Giving him a smirk to show that she understood he was teasing her, Mary looked him in the eyes. "I am irresistible, but sometimes things take longer than I would have thought. Seducing men is a lot easier than seducing women. Most men would crumble within a day should I turn my sights on them; but with women I have needed up to a week to seduce.

"That's why Alexandria is *so* frustrating. I first tried to seduce her a month ago. But no matter how hard I push, how gentle I caress, or how ravishing I am, she still pulls my hands away from her body as we kiss; and if I try again, she pulls away and tells me to leave."

The look of consternation on his twin's face as she vented her frustration over Alexandria made Gabriel smile. "So, you're not as irresistible as you thought." This statement received him an angry glare from his sister, but before she could contradict his assessment, he continued,

"But how does this answer the question about how her rejection of you made you realize that you've been searching for my bride?"

The look Mary was giving him softened from one of anger at his jab at her sexuality, to one of annoyed confusion. Finally looking away from him and back to the ceiling she said, "I don't know. After a week of getting nowhere, I tried something I've never tried before: I brought my friend Simon to try and seduce her for me." It was here that Gabriel noticed the tear at the edge of her eye, and he knew that Simon had been in that field the night before last. "Simon got her to go further than I did, but still our clothes stayed on. And that's when I had my epiphany.

"For as frustrated as I was that this girl would not succumb to my seductions, and I was throwing everything I had at her, seeing her not even fall prey to Simon's remarkable skills, made me happy. And to be happy at so miserably failing is not something that I'm accustomed to feeling. So, I spent the next few days trying to figure out why failing for the first time at something I considered myself an expert in, was making me so happy.

"And that's when I saw you." Gabriel was shocked by what his sister was saying. How was he the key to her realization, when he didn't even know she'd had it until the night before. Turning to look back at him, Mary continued, "I saw you sitting in the library reading some scroll, oblivious to the rest of the world around you. Until Alexandria walked by. I swear to God that you stiffened like a board as she walked past you. And when she turned to see what you were reading, I could feel the nervous beating of your heart from across the building. Seeing the two of you together, was like Moses finding the burning bush; it wasn't something I actively sought, but there it was all the same: the hand of God, showing me the path."

Gabriel couldn't believe the irony of his sister's words. That God would reveal such a thing to such an unrepentant sinner, that her sins had a greater purpose, was comically absurd. But then again, Paul had been quite the sinner as Saul, so maybe the idea wasn't as farfetched as he first thought. "So, actually seeing in person that I liked this girl, was what made you realize this is what you were doing all these years?"

"Don't laugh, I'm being serious!" Mary said in indignation. "I was given an epiphany by God, shown that there was a purpose to my supposed sins, to help my twin brother find love! Ever since that moment of realization, I've gone over every seduction in my mind a hundred times each. I review how I seduced each girl, how attractive and homely she was, what they were like in bed, the amount of effort it took to get them to bed me. I've watched and studied you as if I was going to seduce you myself, seeing what you were attracted to, what turned you off. And then comparing all of this information against itself and my failures regarding Alexandria. This has become a large part of my life, finding the perfect woman for you, Gabriel. Please don't mock it out loud or in your mind."

"I didn't mean to hurt your feelings, Mary," he said contritely, looking into her eyes. "I just thought it was funny that of all the people to receive such a Heavenly mandate, it would be someone who has never put much stock in the previous mandates of Heaven. Surely you can agree with that."

"Thank you, Gabriel, it means a lot that you can believe this load of dung," Mary said with a teasing smile. "The whole 'seeing you was what made me realize this' was a lie." Gabriel couldn't believe it: she'd been so authentic. She was laughing at his confusion as she continued, "I'm sorry, bother dear, but I honestly couldn't resist." Here she couldn't contain her gentle laughing. But upon seeing his serious face, she reined herself in. "Sorry. But to properly answer your question, I don't really know what it was about Alexandria's rejection of my advances that made me realize that what I'd been doing for the past five years was, in part, trying to find you a bride. It came to me a couple of weeks ago as I was taking a bath, randomly, out of the blue. Everything I just said is true, apart from the fact that seeing your crush on Alexandria is what made me realize all this. I've spent countless hours evaluating every female I've seduced over the years, comparing and contrasting them, ranking them in different metrics. I've studied you, the girls your gaze has lingered on, where that gaze has lingered when you think they aren't watching you. I've run through everything me and Simon did to Alexandria to try and seduce her, and her reactions to it all. I've watched her as she goes about her day, hoping that she'll do something that will give me some sort of edge in this game. But all I get is the same diagnosis as before: virtuous, yet lustful."

As she'd gone on about how this had consumed her recent days, Mary had once again turned onto her side. The anger and confusion that rolled off her was starting to even make Gabriel annoyed that this girl was being so stubborn. "Have you ever just asked her why she constantly denies your advances?" he asked. "I mean, this is clearly a sore spot in how you view yourself; so why not take the plunge and just ask Alexandria why, and get the answers you're so desperate for."

Sitting up at the edge of the bed, Mary pulled Gabriel up with her as she looked into his eyes. "Between the time of my epiphany and the fiftieth time I tried to organize all this information in my head, I tried to seduce her again. And after she slapped my hand from her breast for the third time, I snapped and asked her that very question. You need to understand, me asking her that was equivalent to me admitting defeat, and you know how much I hate to lose. So, you can imagine when she just laughed at the question and simply answered 'you're not the one I want' how annoyed I was. The only reason I didn't kill her on the spot was because the next words out of her mouth were quite lavish praise for both my talent in seduction and my alluring assets that have made all previous seductions much easier." Standing up and beginning to pace so as to alleviate the stress reliving this memory was clearly causing her, Mary continued, "She said that she was saving herself for her future husband, sent to her by the Parcae. She claimed that she'd had a vision from Apollo that her future husband would want her pure. And as much as the both of us wanted to have her give in, she said that to deny the warning of a god such as him, would be a grave mistake. Like I said, she's virtuous, yet lustful: she wants to give in, but she's pious enough to obey her gods."

Upon hearing his sister's evaluation of the girl he'd long had a crush on, Gabriel felt his infatuation deepen. To be able to resist the talents of both his sister and her claimed male equal, in the name of faith, was something that he had to admire. In truth, this display of piety from Alexandria only served to heighten his attraction to her. "And now you think that this future husband could, and should, be me?" he asked his twin, stopping her pacing.

Turning to look at him, Mary had a smile mischievously pulling at her lips. "Considering your opinion in the matter, I'd say what I think doesn't really matter. The question is, Gabriel, would you be willing to invoke father's wrath at the mere mention of you're being betrothed to a heathen? For it would surely put his anger at me to shame, for his pride and joy, his perfect son, to come to him and request that he be married to someone outside the faith. Not to mention the daughter of Elder Antonius, whom father despises most of all. Yes, Gabriel, what I think is irrelevant; it's what you're willing to do that matters." Mary looked at him with a gentleness that seemed to convey her truthfulness to him, showing that she meant well with all she'd said. "That is of course, assuming that she and her father accept your proposal." Now her face was full of mirth. "Does she even know who you are? Have you ever talked to her for more than five seconds?"

Despite knowing that Mary was just trying to tease him, Gabriel felt himself blush at her questions. Turning himself away from her mocking gaze, he wracked his brain for any memory that involved Alexandria and himself talking. And to his horror, he couldn't recall any instance that the two of them had had exchanged more than just simple pleasantries. Out of the corner of his eye he saw Mary's smile widen as she came to sit beside him once more. "She knows who I am," he defended weakly.

Taking his hand into hers, Mary laughed at his feeble attempt to not have his ego damaged. When he turned away from her, he felt her tug his hand up and then felt her gently kiss his knuckles. "I really do enjoy the fact that you are so easy to tease, brother. It almost makes me feel normal, laughing at you. But keep your pride in check. In my research over the past few weeks, I have observed you and Alexandria together and unless my eyes are deceiving me, I'd say that she would not be opposed to you being her husband."

Gabriel couldn't hide the quickness that both his head and eyes turned to gaze upon his sister as she said this. There was no sense in denying that she now had his fullest attention. As he stared into Mary's eyes, he tried to judge the authenticity of her words. "Are you serious? Alexandria has a crush on me?"

His twin's gaze didn't falter. "I wouldn't necessarily call it a crush. Like many girls in this town, she finds you attractive. One thing that I've learned about Alexandria is that she's a huntress; she likes to chase after that which catches her eye. And you've certainly done that, Gabriel. You may not realize it, but to the women of this town, you're a bit of an enigma. You believe in Christ, yet you constantly read and reread texts that father condemns for their use of the pagan pantheon; you claim to be an open book, but have little to no friends and prefer for others to leave you alone. People know of you, not know you, and to someone like Alexandria, that's like an invitation to try and discover more. She wants to solve the mystery that is you; but for what it's worth, I think that once she does, she will be attracted to you. You're kind, intelligent and have a good sense of humor, add in your physical attractiveness and you're nearly perfect."

The sincerity with which Mary spoke caused Gabriel to blush. No girl, sister or not, had ever complimented him so. "That's the nicest thing that anyone has ever said to me. Thank you, Mary; it somehow means more coming from you."

Mary just bowed her head in recognition to his thanks. "You're welcome. But before we go trying to get you wed, we have a few more pressing matters to deal with first." The sudden change in subject caught Gabriel off guard, as did the seriousness of his sister's tone. "We need to figure out what the curse the witches at the edge of town placed upon us entails, as well as how to stop it. We can't have us running around town and killing everyone until someone kills us to make it stop. And it's here that I need to have the awkward conversation of weaponizing your crush on that Medea girl."

"We just spent the last twenty minutes discussing my crush on a girl, and now you want to discuss my supposed crush on someone you insist is one of the witches who cursed us. I don't have a crush on Medea," Gabriel tried to rationalize, but felt his voice die away as he saw his twin shake her head.

"Do not think that I don't know you brother. I've spent as much time over the past few weeks watching you and devising seduction plans meant to tempt you as I have with Alexandria. I can tell that you have a crush on that girl from the brief glimpses I caught of the two of you together yesterday, loathe as I am to admit it. And while I do not approve, I can't say I blame you. She's quite beautiful herself, and if what you told us yesterday was the truth, she appears to be plenty intelligent to attract you to her."

Taking a pause to ensure that he was looking into her eyes, Gabriel saw how serious Mary was about all this as she continued. "You have a crush on that girl; granted not as strong as your one on Alexandria, but nothing ever eclipses your first love." Gabriel wanted to argue this point, but as Mary continued, he knew it would be pointless to see if he could convince them both that Alexandria wasn't his first love. "But I don't need you to be in love for my plan to work." At his puzzled expression, Mary gave a simple smile. "When I told mother last night that the look she gave you before kissing you looked like she was judging you, that was a lie. I know what the look in her eyes was and what it means all too well. She was imagining what it would be like to have sex with you, and she wasn't repulsed in the slightest. And now, dear brother, I want you to seduce the truth of all this from her."

Chapter 16
The Beaten

Thunder rolled in the distance as Medea slowed her stride. For as much as she enjoyed the fullness of her powers being hers to control at long last, she was still finding it hard to get a grasp of all that she was now capable of. But the ability to travel distances in the blink of an eye was something that she'd long envied her mother and grandmother for.

As she looked upon the tree that hid her home from the world, Medea took a moment to calm herself. Her conversation with the preacher's son, Gabriel, had left her with much to mull over in her mind. True, the encounter hadn't gone the way she'd hoped; but she wasn't even sure how she wanted it to go, although being interrupted by the boy's jealous sister was not part of the plan. This was all getting out of hand.

With a cleansing breath, Medea walked through the tree trunk that was the door to her home. If she didn't know better, she'd have thought that no time had passed from when she was last in the circular, central room. Her mother and grandmother were both still sitting around the table, the only difference was now that there was a single lit candle between them. Her mother had scried her; or at least had been trying to, she hadn't been gone that long after all.

"As beautiful as you are Medea, I do not believe that you would have been successful in seducing the Iracundus boy so quickly," Hecate taunted from her chair, without even looking to Medea.

"That's because she didn't even try," her mother answered, a look of darkest fury that would have given even Tisiphone pause on her face. "She kissed him and then ran away."

"And what else did you see in your flames, mother?" Medea asked in a harsh tone. "Did you see that his sister came out and interrupted me from even starting my task. Did you see that he gave chase as I ran away? Or did your misplaced and pointless anger make you lose focus? Of course I didn't seduce him in barely two hours; his faith will take time to crack before I can even think to try."

"Your insolence grows more and more grating. Just because you have full access to your powers now, does not give you the right to question your mother or me in such manners," her grandmother scolded, turning to Medea at last with a look that matched her daughter's.

But despite the clear warning in her grandmother's tone and words, Medea had had enough of being their whipping girl. "Call me insolent all you want; it doesn't change the fact that I'm the only one trying to do something to have both our revenge fulfilled and our coven's next generation born while still being able to perform the ancient rites of power and succession! Unless, of course, you've come up with a better plan?" she asked mockingly as she looked to both her mother and grandmother. When after a moment they gave her no response but their continued glares, Medea gave a sneer of a smile. "As I thought, you were so preoccupied with spying on me that you didn't even bother to try and see if my daughter could have the haunting pleasure that is killing her sire."

Without waiting for their response, which would undoubtedly involve beating her, Medea ascended the stairs and threw herself into the room that held the washbasin. Throwing up a barrier to ensure that Hecate and Circe couldn't interrupt her, Medea turned to find her reflection in the mirror. And upon seeing herself, her composure finally broke. The tears that had been knocking at her eyes since her mother told her that she was to meet her father and immediately kill him were finally allowed to fall down her face. This was all becoming too much for her.

She didn't think that killing her father was a pleasure. It was something that would haunt her for the rest of her life, however short that turned out to be. She had long ago forgiven herself for killing the people she had, but Lucius was different; he was her father. The fact that she'd longed to have him in her life was one of her greatest desires; so, to have their brief time together turn out the way it did was heartbreaking. And to have been so dispassionate in killing him, with such little fanfare as if he were nothing but a dog sacrificed to Trivia, was cruelest of all.

Medea's private contemplation was suddenly interrupted by the banging on the room's door and the harshness of her mother's voice. "Medea! You open this door this instant, or so help me, not even Vulcan will be able to put you back together!"

This threat caught Medea off guard; for her mother to invoke a god rather than a goddess was a rare occurrence, rarer still when made in anger. The fact that she'd not only threatened to kill Medea, but claim the god of the forge wouldn't be able to put her back together once her mother was through, was slightly worrying for the girl. Both her mother and grandmother had threatened to kill her in the past, a pastime that had become more engaged in in recent years, but this was perhaps the first time that Medea had ever taken the words seriously.

And it was for this reason alone that she opened the door.

If she had thought that her mother's expression when she arrived home was furious, she clearly didn't know the meaning of the word. The monstrosity that was her mother's face now looked as if all the Irae and Furores had decided to inhabit it all at once. Eyes livid. Nostrils flared. Brows furrowed. Lips snarling. Skin crimson. Muscles tensed. In a word terrifying. Circe's visage drained all the courage and bravado that her daughter had seemed to have built up since she'd returned earlier that day from killing her father.

Involuntarily stepping back as her mother stalked forward toward her, Medea couldn't help the whimpers of fear that escaped her mouth. She tried not to, but she couldn't help but flinch as her mother raised her right hand menacingly. *SMACK*! The force of her mother's palm slapping her face toppled Medea into the mirror, nearly dislodging it from the wall.

Medea had learned long ago to not try to comfort herself when either Hecate or Circe were disciplining her, but the fact that she felt droplets of blood slowly slide down her cheek in the wake of her mother's fingernails, made her raise her hand to her face to confirm her senses. Looking from her fingertips, now stained red, to her mother's face, Medea realized her mistake too late. The backhanded slap rose up diagonally from the middle of her jaw, across her cheek, and ending on the bridge of her nose. The momentum from the impact sent Medea twirling into the tub, the edge of which caught her in the stomach and forced what breath there was in her lungs out.

Half pulling, half pushing herself to a standing position at the tub's side, Medea turned to face her mother, as the coppery taste of blood wetted her taste buds. For the moment she was safe; her mother being a shade farther than an arm's length away. The fury hadn't left her mother's face from when she'd opened the door; in fact, she looked even angrier. As Circe took a step toward her, Medea tried to step back but was blocked by the tub that she was still leaning against as she tried to regain her breath.

"Why mother?" she feebly asked in between pants. "Why do you hate me so? What did I ever do, what did I ever say, to make you treat me worse than you ever treated the preacher and his family? Why don't you love me?" Medea knew that this wasn't the time to ask these questions, questions the son of said preacher had wormed into her brain. But she couldn't help the flicker of hope she felt that asking her mother these questions would snap her out of her rage, and the woman who had comforted her in her anguish at having to kill her own father the previous night would appear.

But hope had never served Medea well.

And today was no different. Her flicker of hope had grown just the slightest as her questions seemed to cause her mother to stop in her tracks for the briefest of moments; her look of pure wrath, stilled and relaxed for the tiniest of seconds. But then it returned and Circe lunged at Medea, her talon-like fingers clawing at the girl's skull as she was dragged from the room, and back downstairs. And as she looked up to her grandmother, silently praying to Juno for relief, Medea felt her blood freeze as Hecate glared down upon her with the same expression of fury as Medea's mother.

And then her discipline began in earnest.

*

Medea awoke to find herself outside, bent into a tangle of odd angles, her dress torn in a dozen or so places and barely holding itself together in a manner that it was still recognizable as a dress, and the noonday sun blazing down on her in a blinding fashion. Unable to move to cover her eyes from the harsh white light that fell upon her, Medea tried to clear her head. From the fact that she was so numb, she knew that more than one bone was broken, not to mention burns from the intense sun on her exposed and cut skin. As she gingerly stretched herself flat onto her back, only moving a single piece of her body at a time, Medea took stock of herself and the injuries her latest session of discipline from her mother and grandmother had provided.

Both her elbows were caked in blood, as was her stomach, left breast and thigh, and her right foot. She knew her face would be too, but she didn't want to know the extent to which she'd be beaten there just yet. Her right nipple, both arms, the soles of her feet, and a strip across her left side that ran from her ribs down to the upper portion of her buttocks had painful sunburns. She could feel the burn on her head as well, along her hairline and roots. Her right arm was broken in three places, two in the forearm and one in the bicep; as was her pinkies, left thumb, five ribs, tailbone and her right foot. Her left shoulder was dislocated, her bottom lip was split on both sides, three teeth were missing and both eyes were nearly swollen shut. She also had countless tiny cuts from where her body had been thrown out by her mother after her and Hecate had finished their lessons the previous night. At least, Medea hoped it had only been a single night.

But despite all the pain that she was in, Medea focused her energies. Silently calling on the goddess Epione and her daughter Aceso, the girl began the long and arduous process of healing herself. The hours passed, as Medea slowly healed herself; the only way she could tell the passage of time was watching Sol's descent toward the horizon. As more of her body healed, Medea was able to glimpse Diana's bow beginning to appear in the sky behind the branches of the tree that made up her home.

It wasn't until the moonlight was being blocked by the clouds that she now knew where a bad omen, that Medea felt that she was fully healed. Sitting herself up, she stretched out her limbs, twisting and turning herself every which way to ensure that she was indeed healed completely. Finding nothing still broken, burnt or bruised, Medea stood herself up and turned to her home, a resigned expression on her face.

Walking through the trunk door, she was not surprised to find her mother and grandmother sitting at the table, her mother's scrying candle once again lit. Medea found it both extremely annoying, as well as amusing, that they would resort to such difficulty just to spy on her when she was just outside. She was just about to tell them off for wasting their time and energies when her grandmother spoke. "What is the demon doing Circe? Why hasn't it killed the family yet? You said that you instructed it to kill the Iracundus family; but so far, it's only turned an orgy into a blood bath. You begged me to entrust you with this most important task, so why do I feel as if that has backfired? Just like trusting you to instill proper respect in your daughter!" The tone with which Hecate demeaned Circe was one Medea had heard often, but it was usually directed toward her rather than her mother. Medea held herself back, hoping to see more of the rare event of her mother being taken down a peg.

Her moment of enjoyment however, was not to be very long. As her mother focused once more on her surroundings, rather than what the candle's flame had shown her, to respond to her mother, she spotted Medea. "The demon seems to be taking an unorthodox approach to its strategy: killing those that the Iracundus family deems to be sinners, painting them as the prime suspects in their murders, before killing them. It's quite clever actually; it may actually undo all that they have done to this town. And please do not remind me of my daughter's failings; seeing her before me is reminder enough." There was a look of venom in her mother's eyes as she glared at Medea, that the girl had to force herself to ignore and not let the hurt it caused in her to reveal itself.

Without looking to her, her grandmother spoke to Medea. "About time you came to your senses girl. Sit," she said pointing to the empty chair. "We must commune with the demon, and we will need your power as well, if we are to be able to use the candle."

Chapter 17
The Demon

My Mistress is angry.

There seemed to be a problem with the plan. She wanted me to both kill the family faster, while at the same time wait to kill the eldest son. Which was absurd; the boy was the pinnacle of what she hated; he was the golden child in the family's eyes. I longed to kill him on simple principle alone: killing him would cause the family the most pain; and it was the community's suffering that had truly been missing in my new life. When I lived, I could almost feed on the despair that surrounded a town in my wake; it was bad enough that this pathetic serpentine body didn't allow for me to feel the life and blood drain from my victims' bodies, but to be unable to enjoy the pleasures that made all this the high it was when I lived was almost insultingly disrespectful.

But, despite all that, I was still ever eager and happy to serve my Goddess, and those she deemed worthy of her gifts.

After my Mistress told me what I should do, I returned to the younger son's room. Sliding myself up onto the bed, I glared upon my prey. He was about the age I was when I first discovered this thrill, the first time I felt the warm splash of blood across my face. I can still see the look of fear in my mother's eyes. A shiver that had nothing to do with my slithering up his body ran through me. I raised myself up high from the boy's chest, thinking myself a cobra rather than the harmless cat snake I was, fangs bared as a hiss escaped my throat, and lunged myself upon his. He struggled and I could feel the sweet spray of his blood in my mouth.

Once again, I felt the phantom sensation of his limbs, now mine to control. My mind was filled with the sights from his eyes. The rush of panicked adrenaline as his body fought the control I had over him fades as my dominance was asserted. Sitting us up, I stretched out his arms, feeling the magic that summoned me back to the land of the living infuse into his weak arms, giving the boy the strength of the great Heracles. I intended to use that strength to make short work of this.

Getting up from the bed, I used the boy's lightness to my advantage as I made my way to the door. The door was easy enough to open, unlike the heavy door of his sister's room meant to keep her from sneaking out at night. The house was dark, but the boy's memories provided me sure footing as we snuck out. But it appeared we weren't the only ones out and about. Sounds of muffled ecstasy can be heard from the main room.

Keeping us to the shadows, I spy a face that I thought looked familiar. A peek into the boy's memories told me he was a neighbor named Julius. It was when he scrunched his face up in concentration that I knew where I'd seen him before. I was about to reveal myself to dispatch of this neighbor and the boy's lying sister when the faintest creak of a door frame brought my attention back to the darkness behind us.

Hiding under a table in the darkness, I await the reveal of the noise maker. I almost lose my grip on the boy's thoughts and neck, for in the sliver of moonlight from the atrium's open ceiling, was his sister. Silently, the girl followed the trail that we'd just walked, seeming to be drawn to the coupling occurring in the other room. Staying out of the candle light that poured out, the girl watched with a look both sad and hungry on her face. But as clearly as she wanted to interrupt the neighbor and her mother, the sister silently walked to the house's main entrance and snuck herself away.

Tempted to follow her out, I start to crawl us out from under the table. It was only when the mother's cry of euphoria brought my attention back to the other room that I had a wicked thought. Turning my attention back to the adulterous pair in the main room, I decide to engage in one of my favorite pastimes from when I lived. Honestly, the orgy massacre had reminded me how much fun it was to scare lovers in the midst of their amorous activities.

But where the other night had allowed for me to once again indulge Lovers Hunt, it was truly lacking the suspicious fear that always added a fun taste to the atmosphere. Now, was a perfect time to try and play as best I could with the boy's small and quick body to an even better effect. And with that in mind, I walked us quickly and quietly as we could back to the boy's room.

It was here that I pulled open the door to his room; the creak would have been innocuous during the day, but when you're cheating on your spouse in the dead of the night, any sound could spell you end. There's a definitive pause in the action as they both seem to try and listen for anything that indicated that they needed to stop. As I hear them resuming, I walk the boy back toward the main room and purposely bumped into a table. Another pause as I hear the muffled mother demand the neighbor come out and see what was causing the racket. Hiding beneath the table I'd just bumped, I could see the neighbor come to the room's entrance as he looked out to find the source of the disturbances.

I follow at a distance as he returns to his lover and began taking her from behind. It was only a moment before the two were too engrossed in their activities to notice us as I sneak up behind them. I wait until he was just about to finish before I shove the boy's hand through the neighbor's back. I feel the ghostly impact the boy's hand has on Julius' body: the shattering of both spine and ribs, the ripping of muscle and lungs, the *warmth* of his blood. But most of all, as I use the boy's puny arm to hold the heart on the other side of his chest, I get to feel it: the final beats of his heart. Starting strong, as though it still thought it was in its body, but then fading as it pumped blood out and down the tiny fingers that held it.

I squeeze the last of the blood out of the heart like it was a wet rag. As I pull back the boy's arm, crushed heart still in hand, the adulterous neighbor's body slumped to the floor with a wet thud. And that's when the mother realizes something is wrong. Turning she sees her baby boy, covered in the blood of her lover with said lover's heart in her son's hand. She was about to let out a scream as I jump up and straddle her, shoving the heart into her mouth to prevent any sound.

Using the bloody hand, I bring a finger to the boy's lips. "Shhh, Mommy Dearest." I can hear the sound of my voice overlay the boy's, creating a deliciously disturbing contrast. "We wouldn't want Daddy to come and see you whoring about with the neighbor, now would we. But don't worry, we're going to have some bonding time for just the two of us," I say with a wicked smile. Picking up her discarded dress, I rip a strip off and tie it around her head, securing the heart in place as a gag. I'm about to throw the dress back down, but see a pin holding a lapel in place. Taking it out, I rip the thin needle from the pin. "Now, Mommy, we are going to have some fun."

I was surprised that in the hour that I'd taken to have such delicious fun with the family's matriarch that the boy's sister hadn't come home. So, I had decided to go out and find her. I had just finished setting the scene for discovery, when the family servant came into the room. Knowing that I had to act quickly, I leapt at him and climbed up him until the boy's body sat on his shoulders. With a practiced hand, I snap his neck.

When I lived, I always hated these kills, the quick to ensure I wasn't caught. But in all honesty, I felt a swell of nostalgia at the act. As I let that wave wash over me for a moment, I quickly decide what to do with this added complication. Stripping him, I drag him over to the neighbor's body, and position it like the two were being intimate. Having listened to the insufferable ramblings about this new god that the father had given the other day in the square, I knew the concept of the two men in 'bed' together would add to his misery at all this.

With a final look to the tableau of my work, I set off into the night, searching for the boy's sister. Using my superior strength, I climb us up the walls of the house and leap from roof to roof. I search for nearly half an hour as I look for the boy's whore of a sister. I'm just about to give up and return to the home when I find her. Hiding in an alleyway on the opposite side of town, it appears that her ruse of being repentant at her whorish behavior was all an act. With her is a boy about her age, taking her against the wall. She really is her mother's daughter

Since I have been given this wonderful opportunity to play Lovers Hunt once again, I take the opportunity with glee. From the roof above, I drop a couple pebbles and sediment from the building's wall. In the pause I hear the boy say he's so strong that he's breaking the wall; I laugh internally at this, the boy's a twig. I jump across the alley with the supernatural power that now runs through the boy's limbs. Scaling down the building on the opposite side, I step loudly to ensure they hear the approach of someone. Their moaning stops as I draw closer, and I hear the sound of one of them come to check the square at the mouth of the alleyway. Hiding us behind a stand, I spy the twig look about for any sign of another person before returning to the sister.

Quiet as a mouse, I follow him down the alley, keeping to the shadows to ensure they don't see me coming. It's only when I see and hear them re-engage their coupling that I make my move. As the boy's body is too small to attack from this angle, I once again climb the wall bringing myself parallel with the boy. Since I'd ripped out a heart already tonight, I aim higher. Smashing through his spine, I wrap the phantom physical fingers around his throat and pull it out.

As the sister's lover's body slumps to the ground with a sickening crunch, I expect her to cry out. Instead, something I've never encountered happens: she closes her eyes and stands tall. My surprise causes me to hesitate. And that hesitation allows for the girl to speak.

She begs.

But unlike all my victims, she isn't begging for her life. Stranger still, she seems to be begging to me and not her brother. She begs me to let him go, that he shouldn't have these memories. She accepts that she's to die, but her brother shouldn't have to live with the memory of killing his own sister.

"Fret not, girl, he won't live long enough to be undone by this memory," I reassure as I place my blood-soaked hands upon her face. The second person I ever killed was someone who was basically a disciple of my killing. Barely sixteen, she treated me like a god; she claimed that she loved me, that she'd fallen in love with me when she witnessed me kill my mother. She begged me to let her bring me victims, even offering her own betrothed and her first born. Hers was a gentle death, the gentlest I'd ever given.

And that's what I gave the sister.

Chapter 18
The Banished

As she gazed into the candle's flame, Medea felt a tear threaten to fall down her cheek. She didn't know why, but something about the way the demon had killed the girl made her sad. The gentleness, when everything else had been so visceral and carnage-filled; whatever it was that the girl had said to the demon had moved it, and she now needed to know what it was she said.

The flickering of the flame brought Medea back to her immediate surroundings. Trying to refocus herself, Medea concentrated her thoughts on seeing the movements of the demon. She watched as it returned to the Iracundus home, returning the boy to his bed to await his family's discovery of the adulterous scene in the main room. Medea was slightly disgusted by the care the demon had seemed to put into staging the scene; although she knew that it would be quite effective.

She watched the candle flame flicker for five more minutes before she let her concentration wane and her awareness return to her own surroundings. "It's clearly going to wait until morning for the others to discover the new damage," she told her mother and grandmother as they looked to her.

"It should finish off the family ton—"

"I still need to seduce the son so as to further our line," Medea interrupted her grandmother. "Besides, the demon needs to be allowed to enact its plan to have the town turn on the family; the Iracunduses would only be martyred if they all died at once. Those that they deem as sinners have been expunged from their family, and the way the demon has staged their bodies will draw suspicion upon the patriarch. We summoned the demon to do more than just kill them, we summoned it to enact our revenge; and what better revenge can there be than not only killing them, but framing them for their own murders, and in so doing, undo all that they've worked to achieve by converting this town from the gods to theirs."

"You can't deny the irony, and genius, of that plan, mother," Circe begrudgingly interjected before Hecate could berate Medea for interrupting her.

"Silence, you insolent children!" her grandmother shouted, causing even Circe to bow contritely. "I grow tired of the two of you telling me what I have to do. I am the matriarch of this family, my word is law; and I say for you to have the demon finish the job we summoned it for and kill the rest of that accursed family!"

Sitting herself down beside Medea, her mother responded by staring intently into the scrying candle. But as her mother sat, Medea stood. "Have you forgotten the visions sent to me by Trivia and Terra? We can't kill them all if we wish for our family to take advantage of their absence and continue into the next generation."

"That is, if you're telling the truth," Hecate said in a deadly calm. "Sit your worthless, lying ass down, girl." Medea did so out of fear that her deception had been discovered. "I've been asking myself why the gods would allow such a colossal oversight to occur; but they wouldn't. You Medea, on the other hand, have been against this plan form the beginning. So, what seems more likely: the gods messed up, or that you're lying about the Iracundus boy being your mate?"

Medea's mind raced as she tried to think of how to talk her way out of this corner that she'd walked herself into. She knew that she had to be convincing, as even Circe had abandoned the attempt to scry the demon and turned her full attention on her daughter. "Why would I lie about something so important as this, the father of my daughter? What would I gain by lying? You're right that I haven't always been fully on board with the plan to kill the Iracundus family, but I've never denied that something needed to be done. They turned our neighbors against us simply for practicing our faith because it was different from theirs; something we did in peace." She'd glared into her grandmother's eyes, daring her to call her bluff. Where this confidence was coming from, she didn't know. "If it were up to me, the Iracundus boy wouldn't be destined to be my mate; I'd want someone not from here, someone who practiced my faith. I'm being punished by this blunder as well."

"Liar," Hecate rasped. "Your coming into your powers made it difficult to read, but now I know, you've not said a word of truth about this whole situation since you killed your sire." Suddenly, Medea was pulled from her chair and found herself in her grandmother's choking hand, the lead sickle still stained with her father's blood pressed just below her eye. "Tell me the truth now, Medea," she snarled at her granddaughter. "Who is *really* meant to father your daughter?"

The hand that held her throat loosened the slightest bit to allow her to squeak the faintest of answers out. "No one."

Whatever her grandmother had been expecting, it clearly wasn't that, as Hecate's grip on Medea completely loosened as the girl dropped to the floor. "What do you mean 'no one'?"

Coughing as she tried to regain enough air to breathe, Medea glared up at her grandmother. "What's there to explain, it's fairly self-explanatory. When I performed the ritual, darkness clouded my mind and formed into the silhouette of a face. But before any clarity could be given, the darkness dissipated. So, unless Scotus himself is breeding me, according to the gods, no one is."

Medea's gaze shifted between both her mother's and grandmother's as she revealed this. But the fury she expected to find in their eyes was not there; there was no emotion in the eyes of her elders. That was until her mother let out a deep pitying sigh. "And that, daughter, was the final straw," Circe said quietly into the stillness, cutting it sharply.

As one, her mother and grandmother began to circle Medea, left hands raised to their neck level and arms bent. Similar to when they had summoned the demon, her mother and grandmother chanted in unison, but where before their circling had meant to contain the magic unleashed, they now sought to unleash it. "*We unbind you, Unclean One!*

We strip you of your power, and reclaim it for our own. Be gone, Unclean One; you are no longer one of us!"

As they circled Medea four times, continuously chanting, she felt the power that she'd only just started to get used to surging through her be drained away. As her mother and grandmother finished magically removing Medea from their coven, she felt her body start to weaken, and she had to fling herself to the table to stay standing. "Get out of my house, traitor," Hecate scowled. "You are no longer one of us, and therefore are no longer welcome here. Be thankful that all we've done is stripped you of your magic and not killed you as we should. The blood we share is all that keeps you from death; but should you ever see my or my daughter's face again, you shall die."

Hardly able to hold herself upright, Medea tried to walk to the door as steadily as she could. But having her power forcibly taken from her had left her weaker than she thought she'd ever be, and it wasn't even five steps before Medea's legs gave out. Utterly humiliated and heartbroken, the girl started to cry quietly as she crawled the rest of the way to the door. But for as cruel and heartless as her mother and grandmother could be, Medea was forever grateful that they didn't laugh or taunt her as she pulled herself out of the only home she'd ever known.

But as she came to the threshold of the tree that had been her home, she pulled herself upright. And even though her legs were still shaky and weak, Medea forced herself to walk out with her head held high. The shrouded moon gave little light, but she didn't need to see to know where she was going. She kept a picture of the simple, if slightly larger than most, home in her mind as she took each step. Whether her strength was returning or Terra had taken pity on her and was giving her strength, she didn't know, but as she walked away from her ancestral home, Medea could feel her feet were firmer upon the ground. By the time she'd reached the hidden boarder that kept out all magic except that of the family's coven, Medea was able to run; and run she did. The thought of the Iracundus home, the only thought in her mind, she raced toward town and her enemies.

And then thunder rolled.

Chapter 19
The New Patriarch

"Please, Gabriel, wake up," the voice that shook him awake shakily demanded.

Thinking it was Mary seeking his comfort from a nightmare, he turned himself onto his back. "Just snuggle up, Mary. It's too early to talk," Gabriel mumbled.

"I'm not your sister," the weak voice said, startling him awake.

From the little light that came in from the window, Gabriel, now awake, recognized the form of the girl that had caused his sister to feel jealous: Medea. She was bent over, with a hand on her stomach and the other on the bed, seeming to keep her upright. Sitting himself up, Gabriel looked to her with concern as he realized that she was in pain. "What's wrong, Medea? How and why are you here?"

"We have to go. There's not much time. Help me find your father; the two of you need to leave now." Medea was trying to drag him out of bed to the door as she avoided answering him. "Come on, Gabriel! Before my mother and grandmother wake the demon and send him here to kill you!"

"Medea stop!" he said as he pulled himself free of her grip. "What's going on? And what do you mean that your mother and grandmother are going to send a demon to kill me? And why are you only concerned about me and my father? Is the rest of my family safe?"

"The rest of your family is dead. Your mother, her lover and your family servant are in the main room displayed in a way that you shouldn't see; your sister is an alley near the market on the other side of town, with a lover of her own and her neck snapped. As for your brother, he's the one possessed by the demon and the one on the hunt to kill you and your father, and should my mother learn that I'm here, he'll probably be told to kill me as well. I'm sorry for having to tell you this, but now is not the time for niceties, it's the time to run away." There was a look that was both sorrowful and annoyed upon the girl's face. She, in some form of sympathy, was trying to do what she thought to be right.

"My family's dead?" he asked in a hollow voice.

Stepping in close to him, Medea slapped Gabriel across the face with an effort that seemed to take more out of her than he would have thought necessary for such a simple act. "Run now, mourn later," she said as she grabbed his toga and started to drag him toward the door.

Planting his feet and gently shoving her hand off him, Gabriel saw the girl drop against the door, causing it to close with a bang that rang throughout the quiet house. Seeing Medea seeming to crumble to the ground, Gabriel forgot the outburst he was about to have at her and dropped down to see if she was alright. "You're hurt; co—"

"I'm weak, not hurt. Now, please Gabriel, let's wake your father and get as far from here as we can. Once we're on our way, I promise, I'll explain everything you wish to know. So, can we please hurry?" Medea had pulled herself up as she spoke.

She was about to open the door, when there was a knock from the other side. "Gabriel, who are you talking to? And what are you doing up at such an hour? And what was that bang?" his father asked from the other side of the door. Medea threw the door open to reveal his father with a candle in hand. "Gabriel! Why is this strange woman in your room?" his father asked in an angry voice. Gabriel couldn't really blame him, this was behavior that Mary was famous for, not him.

"She's trying to save your lives," Medea answered his father. Then she pushed herself from the door frame, attempting to leave. "We need to leave now, bef—"

"Father, what's going on?" Gabriel heard his brother call from the hallway. Upon hearing his voice, Medea had gone quiet and fear had crept into her eyes as she started to tremble.

"Get in," she hissed at his father, trying to drag him into the room.

But Gabriel's father, like his son before him, flung her arms from himself, causing Medea to fall to the floor. "Keep your hands to yourself, woman." He turned back to the hallway to speak to Marcus II, when a tiny hand burst from his chest. And in it, beating its last beat, was his father's heart.

Gabriel cried out upon feeling the blood that had burst forth from the wound splash against him. But as his father's body slumped to the floor, revealing his brother, heart still in his bloody hand, Gabriel sank to his knees. "That was disappointing," his brother said in a voice that wasn't entirely his own. "I had such fun plans for him." Turning to look at Gabriel, he said, "But, alas, my Mistress now wishes for this to be finished." With a speed unnatural to his brother, Gabriel knelt transfixed as Marcus II came rushing toward him. His bloodied hand rested on Gabriel's chest, no doubt ready to rip his heart out, when Gabriel saw a flicker of an idea pass through his eyes. "You know, it's been so long since I killed a pair of twins together, I'm going to offer you a choice. You can either die like your parents, and have me rip out your beating heart; or, you can die like your whore sister, where I simply snap your neck. Which would you prefer?" his brother asked in that unsettling voice that wasn't his own.

"Why are you offering?" he asked in a vain hope to stall the inevitable. "And my sister wasn't a whore."

His brother gave a harsh laugh at this. "Oh please, boy! Even your brother, who yes is still alive in here, knows she was a whore. She was out fornicating with some twig of a boy when I killed her."

"That wasn't fornication! It was comfort!" Gabriel glared defiantly into the eyes of his brother.

"Comfort?" the boy asked disbelievingly. "I thought you were her comfort." He sneered into Gabriel's face, before another idea flashed behind his eyes. "She came to you for that comfort, didn't she brother? That's why she accepted death so readily; because her true source of comfort had denied her." Gabriel couldn't hide the sting the truth in his words brought out. He'd led his sister and her lover for the night to a grisly death, at the hands of his brother. He felt the tears well up in his eyes. "That's what I thought."

"You never answered my question," Gabriel stated as he turned his face from the triumph that radiated from the demon controlling his brother. Forcing himself to look back to the questioning look of his possessed brother, he asked, "Why are you offering me a choice in how I die?"

"Twins are joined in ways that no one who isn't one can understand," Marcus II said. "I'm simply trying to keep that connection between you and Mary. When I lived and ever came upon a set of twins, I'd always kill them in the same manner. They came into the world together, and though they might not leave it together, they'd leave it the same way. It's almost poetic, right?" Though he hated to admit it, Gabriel did see the poetic symmetry to the demon's point. "So, what's it going to be? Like your twin for poetry, or like your mommy and daddy so I get to feel the last beat of your heart?"

"You already ripped my heart out," Gabriel said to the slight confusion of the demon. "So, I choose poetry." He held his head a little higher to allow the demon that controlled his brother access to his neck to snap it.

With a small smile, the demon said, "Very well." Placing his hands on Gabriel's chin and the back of his head, the demon looked him in the eye. A savageness passed in his brother's eyes as he felt the hands holding his head tense. But when he thought that the demon was going to snap his neck, there was a blinding flash of light. And with a thud, his brother's body lay on the floor.

Gabriel looked to Medea, assuming that she'd down something, afraid that she'd killed his brother. "What did you do?" he demanded of her.

"Just now, nothing. But when I kissed you the other day, I placed a protection spell on you." Seeing his look of confused outrage, she continued, "It simply knocks out your attacker; your brother, and the demon that possesses him, are simply unconscious. But we really need to go now. Before my mother and gran—" The sound of thunder rolling outside caused her to stop. Gabriel saw that Medea was just as terrified of the thunder as she had been of his brother talking in the hall. Seeing that caused him to feel fear well up inside him as well. "I don't suppose you have anything sharp and made of lead that can be quickly attained?"

Slightly confused by this abrupt change in subject, Gabriel gave Medea a confused look. Nodding slightly, he said, "We have a lead sickle out back in my mother's garden." As more thunder rolled and the sound of a hard rain could be heard beginning to smack against the house, he asked, "That's your mother and grandmother, isn't it?"

Ignoring his question, Medea shoved him toward the door. "Get the sickle quickly and quietly. Then get back here and hide as best you can; when their backs are turned, slit their throats. Now go!" She pointed out toward the hall as she knelt face down beside his father as Gabriel ran from the room.

Chapter 20
Medea

Laying down in the Iracundus patriarch's blood, Medea tried to keep herself as still as possible once she heard the house's front doors blow open by the wind. Raindrops fell hard onto the roof and windows, the cacophony of which made listening for approaching footsteps all the harder. Thankfully, her mother and grandmother were not being subtle in their arrival.

"Demon!" she heard her mother's voice call out. "Demon, come here!"

It was here that Medea heard the quiet rustle of wet cloth and bare feet as Gabriel returned to the room. She assumed he'd hid himself as he'd barely returned before Medea could see the unnatural light from Hecate and Circe's runestone flash down the hallway. Trying to draw as much magic as her weakened body could absorb from the ground, Medea forced herself to go slack as she awaited discovery by her former coven.

"Circe! In here!" her grandmother's voice rasped out. Her mother's footsteps were not far from the doorway, but they came to a stop at what she assumed was Hecate's side.

And then there was a wet thud as something fell to the ground.

Feeling the runestone's light shine upon her, Medea heard a gasp as her mother let out a breath, that had it been anyone but her mother, Medea would have sworn it was a cry of shocked anguish. "Medea…" the sorrow of her mother's voice almost made Medea open her eyes to see why her mother was so sad.

"Get up, Circe! That traitorous spawn of yours isn't worth your tears. She was weak and a disgrace." Oddly, Medea didn't hear the wet *shlick* she thought would accompany her mother standing. "Circe!"

"She may have been a worthless traitor, mother, but Medea was still my daughter." If she hadn't have heard it with her own ears, Medea would have never believed it; had her mother just defended her right to *mourn* Medea, and to her grandmother of all people? That was when she felt a gentle brush against her cheek, pushing the stray locks of hair that had covered her face out of the way. "*Goodbye, my daughter. May your power grow as you join the goddesses of our faith.*"

"She does not deserve the rites of our coven, Circe. She is not a part of it. We ban—" Whatever it was her grandmother was going to say was cut short by a thunderous crash that Medea felt in her bones, as the light in the room greatly diminished. As her mother let out a yell of shocked rage, Medea felt something large hit the floor.

"Mother!" Circe cried. "You!" A loud thud accompanied by Gabriel's grunt came from the side of the room. Medea opened her eyes and saw her mother had thrown the boy into the wall a foot off the ground, one hand around his throat while the other pinned the hand that held the lead sickle in it. "That's the second member of my family that you've killed tonight, boy. You'll not get the chance to kill the third," Medea heard her mother snarl up at Gabriel.

With a snap, Circe broke Gabriel's wrist, causing him to drop the sickle to the floor with a dull clang. Silently as she could, confident that her mother was otherwise distracted, Medea pushed herself up and crawled toward the sickle. "The fact that my daughter is lying there proves that she was indeed a traitor; that she had come here to try and save your life. She spends all of an hour talking with you and she is suddenly willing to betray her family and beliefs? What is so important about you, that makes her want to save you? What spell did you place on my daughter that made her fall in love with you?"

Upon hearing her mother's final question, Medea turned to look at Circe in confusion. In her periphery, she saw Gabriel look to Circe with a similar look. Medea flinched at hearing her mother's laughter as she saw the confusion in Gabriel's eyes. She could hear the genuine, yet malicious, smile in her mother's laughter, and it caused Medea to shrink back in fear even more.

"Oh, she didn't tell you?" Gabriel's head shook imperceptibly, causing her mother to give another harsh laugh. "Yes, boy, my daughter was in love with you. She put a protection spell on you and tried to convince me and her grandmother that you were the one meant to father her daughter. Truthfully, I had my suspicions at that; but Terra's plan was apparently to be crueler: that she was to bear no daughter, that our coven would be shattered by your family and our attempted vengeance upon you. Well, I'll not let you escape my justified vengeance!" Circe's voice was once again as Medea remembered it: cold and cruel.

As silently as she could, Medea completed her journey to the fallen sickle that laid just behind her mother's vision. Picking it up, she nearly immediately dropped it at the sight of her grandmother's blood staining the blade. A similar feeling had shuddered through her body as she held the sickle that cut her father's throat; she'd assumed it was her own revulsion at having killed her father. But now Medea knew that wasn't the case, it was her power reacting to a threat in the blades themselves. These sickles had spilled the blood of her close kin, she should be wary of them.

Wrapped in her own thoughts, Medea nearly missed Gabriel's attempt to keep her mother's attention on himself, lest her deception be discovered. "You want to know what me and your daughter talked about?" His voice was barely above a squeak, as Circe's hand only barely relaxed its grip on the Iracundus boy, only just allowing him to breathe and speak. "I gave her advice about how to have a better relationship with you. She told me that she'd had a fight with you and her grandmother, I simply offered my two denarii and told her to find out why the three of you were always fighting. I—"

Gabriel's next words were cut off, as Circe applied more pressure and closed off the boy's airways. "You!" her mother said in a voice so colored in rage that Medea could see the ocean of blood her words would create if they could be made manifest. "You were the one that poisoned her with such thoughts? If I weren't already going to kill you boy as slowly and painful as I intend to, know that corrupting my daughter with such poisonous thoughts would warrant your death to last many weeks." Medea couldn't see her mother's face, but she imagined it looked much like how it looked when she had asked her this question if Gabriel's look of fear was anything to go by. "Luckily for you, I do not have the time to savor this as much as I would like to."

With that said, Circe dropped Gabriel, as she turned to pick up the sickle that now rested in Medea's hands. Gripping and regripping the handle, Medea pointed the sickle down at her mother as she searched for the sickle. When Circe's head snapped up to find the lead sickle pointed at her throat, Medea would have thought she saw a flicker of relief at seeing her alive, but it was probably just shock at finding the deadly weapon held to her throat for in the next moment the terrifying look of fury was once again on her mother's face. "I'm sorry, Mother." The gentle whisper carried in the momentary silence of the storm. Medea didn't know what she was apologizing for, but for whatever it was, she was sorry.

"You are not my daughter. No daughter of mine would so forsake her coven and family." Her mother's dispassionate voice was betrayed by the fierceness with which the storm slammed into the house. Rain battered the roof and walls as if Jove had taken all of Neptune's domain and thrown it all at them. Wind caused the shutters on the windows to blow open so hard that they broke their moorings and fell to the ground and splintered into pieces. Lightning arced across the sky so frequent that her mother's runestone paled in comparison to the light that came from the skies above. Circe's fury had not just brought a storm, it had unleashed Typhaon and the gods had come en masse to reimprison the rampaging father of monsters.

Quicker than Medea thought her capable of, Circe jumped back and had her hand around Gabriel's throat and his body between the two witches acting as a human shield. "Let him go, mother." Medea had to yell to be heard in the storm, despite their close proximity.

"You are not in any position to give me orders, girl," her mother snarled in return. "Not if you want him to live." The fingers around Gabriel's throat flexed so that they looked like a claw rather than her mother's dainty hand. But no matter how small it looked, Medea knew that her mother could rip out Gabriel's throat with just her pinky and thumb if she wanted to.

Stepping the few steps so that she was within arm's reach of Gabriel's chest, Medea kept the lead sickle level with Circe's face as she peaked out from behind the boy's head. "His life is forfeit, mother; he's been living on borrowed time ever since we called forth the demon. But he's not yours to kill." Looking to both Gabriel and her mother, Medea saw the twin looks of apprehension and confusion that her words caused in them. "I'm the one who placed the protection spell on him, I'm the only one who can kill him without ending up unconscious. And once it's done, you can torture and kill me to your heart's content, as you've wanted to do for so many years."

Circe gave a harsh laugh at this. "Do you think that my mother and I taught you everything we know? Or that we never had the power to undo any magic you cast? Your weak heart was on display to us since you could walk, stupid girl, and so we've held the true power of Trivia and

Terra back from you. We hoped that we'd be able to quash the compassion you held for these people out of you, but it appears we failed. You weren't strong when we banished you, and you're even weaker now."

"If I'm so weak, why do you hide behind some boy, especially one you plan to kill yourself?" Medea taunted her mother. She could see the blind fury return to Circe's eyes at her remark and the fact that she'd cut her off. "If beating me is such a simple matter, then why not come out and prove it?" Medea took a couple steps back, making sure to avoid the puddle where the Iracundus patriarch's blood had mixed with the flood of rain water still pouring in from the smashed window, and spread her hands wide to goad her mother to come face her.

With more force than was needed, Circe tossed Gabriel aside, causing him to crash through the wardrobe that he'd hidden in upon Circe and Hecate's arrival. Forcing herself to not look and see if he was alright, Medea locked her eyes on her mother as she approached her in a fury. Swinging her clawed hands out to attack Medea, Circe lunged forwards. But where Medea had been mindful of where she stepped, her mother didn't seem to be, for as she came forward, her momentum caused her to slip on the ground wet with blood and water.

And with the same dispassion she'd used to kill her father, the dispassion her mother had spent her entire life trying to instill in her, Medea flawlessly sliced Circe's throat open. And while the storm faded away almost instantly, thunder boomed deafeningly for another minute. The entire time, Medea watched the hateful fury that radiated out from her mother's eyes, as she spent her last moments surely wishing looks could kill, if only to have a final act of revenge. But as the final crash of thunder rolled and her mother's eyes hateful gaze glazed over, Medea slumped to the ground. Dropping the sickle still sending waves of nausea up her arm to her head and stomach, she crawled like a newborn babe to her mother's body.

Throwing herself over the body, Medea nuzzled herself into her mother's collarbone, where she was still able to feel blood seep out from her cut throat. And then her tears flowed like the rain had only moments before.

Chapter 21
The Friend

As he came to, Gabriel tried to push himself up with his right hand, but the jolt of pain that ran up his arm as he did so, reminded him of his broken wrist. Using his left hand, he grabbed onto the splintered door to the wardrobe that the witch had thrown him through and tried to pull himself to a standing position. He felt lightheaded and had to use the wardrobe to keep himself upright.

Sunlight was starting to come in through the broken windows, allowing for Gabriel to see what had become of his room in the night. The stones that made up the floor were covered in blood, and the entranceway was covered in the bodies supplying said blood. Looking over the bodies of his father, brother and the witches, Gabriel heard the faint sobs of Medea as she clutched herself to her mother's dead body. Feeling steadier on his feet, he pushed himself off the wardrobe and took the few steps to be by her side.

Kneeling down, Gabriel reached out his left hand and started to rub her back. But his touched seemed to startle her, as she flinched away and turned herself to face him so fast that he flinched back in surprise also. When she saw that it was him, she relaxed slightly. Looking at her face,

Gabriel noticed that her eyes were red and puffy and that parts were covered in her mother's blood, while other parts showed the tracks of her tears. "I'm sorry," he said, meaning more than for just scaring her.

Wiping her eyes to try to hide her tears, only succeeded in spreading the half-dried blood on her face. "It's not your fault," she said, seeming to understand his meaning.

Standing up, Gabriel offered her his hand, which she took and allowed him to pull her up and over to his bed. Sitting them down, Gabriel didn't know what to do next. Unable to keep looking at her and seeing the sadness in her eyes, Gabriel once again took stock of the damage and carnage spread across his room. When his eyes found his brother, he asked. "Why isn't my brother awake? You said that we needed to hurry and leave before he came to. Surely it's been hours since all this happened; so why is he still unconscious?" There was a bit of anger laced into his voice, he hoped that she hadn't been lying to him before about his brother being dead.

"The protection spell I placed on you wasn't one based on time, but one based on distance. Your brother is still unconscious because you are still close by, and will remain that way until we remove the demon from him or until the two of you are on opposite sides of town." Gently, she put her hand on his chin and turned his face so he looked upon her. "I'm sorry, too. I know that I'm partly responsible for all this, but I want you to know that I never wanted it. I tried to convince my mother and grandmother to not go through with this plan; I thought it would only make the world see us as the monsters that your father had painted us as. But, like I told you when we first met, I believe that something needed to be done. You may have never seen it, but whenever my family came into town, we were harassed and would have to practically threaten to curse everyone to just accept our business. We just wanted to be able to live our lives in peace, or at least, that's what I wanted. My mother and grandmother were more vindictive and probably would have killed the entire town if they weren't convinced that your father's constant preaching the word of Christ as the only real religion was the source of this inhumane treatment."

Gabriel simply nodded to the girl's apologetic confession. He could understand that her family would feel slighted by this treatment. But despite knowing that some form of action was justified, Gabriel didn't know if he had it in him to forgive Medea her part in the death of his family. Turning to look back at his brother's still unconscious body, he asked, "How do we rid my brother of the demon possessing him and ensure that it returns from wherever you summoned it from?"

"You do what my mother accused you of doing," Medea said cryptically. When he turned back to look at her in confusion, she elaborated. "You kill me. The protection spell I placed on you will dissipate, and both your brother and the demon will wake. But the demon will be severely weakened by the death of those that summoned it, and be unable to continue possessing your brother as it searches for another power source to keep it alive. Once the snake that houses the demon removes itself from your brother, use the lead sickle to cut off its head. The snake will disappear into smoke and sink back to the underworld. Then, to ensure that you, your family or this town never has to suffer my family's magic again, you should burn our house down. There are still plenty of witches and covens in the empire that are resentful over the emperor's renouncement of our faith for Christianity, and we don't want them to discover what my family tried to do to change that fact. Not to mention what they'd do with some other spells and rituals that my family has written down there."

Gabriel was shocked at the lengths and thoroughness that Medea thought were necessary to ensure a complete victory over her family. "Are-are you sure that all that's necessary? It seems like overkill; nobody in town knows where you live so they wouldn't be able to tell anyone where to look beyond simply saying on the outskirts of town."

Shaking her head, Medea said, "Others like me would be able to find it, if they knew to look. It may be overkill, but it's better to be safe than sorry." Standing herself up, she continued, "Come on; grab your brother and let's go."

"I can't—"

"I know you want to stay with your family, but—"

"No, Medea, I mean I can't," he said holding up his broken wrist. "I can't carry Marcus like this, and I don't want you touching him."

He knew that his words had come out harsher than he'd meant them by the look that she gave him as he expressed his unwillingness to have Medea hold his brother. But it was quickly replaced by a sympathetic smile. "Of course; I forgot that my mother did that. Come with me outside, and I'll have you healed in no time," she said as she turned back to the room's entryway and led the way outside.

Following Medea around the bodies of their families, Gabriel allowed her to cover his eyes as they made their way past the atrium. She said it was because he shouldn't see his mother how the demon had left her. He was inclined to believe her. Walking out into the front yard, Gabriel felt the wet grass beneath his feet and he took a second to wiggle his toes in the sensation.

Copying Medea, he sat himself down across from her. Holding her hands together over her lap, she said, "Give me your hand." Gingerly placing his right arm in her cupped hands, Gabriel instantly felt a slight tingle jumping from Medea to himself. "This may take a while to finish; I've never had to heal anyone other than myself before and my magic is severely weakened from what it was the last time I healed myself."

Gabriel nodded his understanding. But despite her warning about it taking some time, he could already feel the pain slipping away and the strange crunch of his bones resetting themselves. It wasn't five minutes before Gabriel could have sworn his wrist was fully healed. But he would wait until Medea said he was finished healing before he removed his hand from hers, just in case she was still fixing some unknown part of him. By the time a half an hour had passed and the sun had risen into the sky over the homes of the town, she lowered her hands back to her sides. "I think that should do it," she said to him. Standing herself up, Medea held up a hand to indicate that Gabriel should stay sitting. "Please," she said in a meek repentant tone. "please allow me a few moments to reposition your mother to a more dignified position. It's bad enough that she died in such a way, but you shouldn't see her like that. The demon posed her in such a way as to bring your father great shame and anger; I don't want you to feel any more negative emotions than you already do."

The look Medea gave him as she requested this was one of pleading. He knew that she was only trying to save him pain, and that was the only reason that he nodded. She'd said that his mother was with a lover, and he did not wish to know who it was. So, he awaited her return outside, feeling the warming sun on his skin as he made his way over to the nook where he often enjoyed reading.

He'd barely sat down when he'd heard a feminine *ahem* from the other side of the stone wall that divided the yard from the street. Looking up, he was shocked to see none other than Alexandria standing across the wall from him. Standing himself up straight, Gabriel took in her beauty. Her hair was the golden brown of wheat and came down in curls to the tops of her medium sized breasts. Her eyes a hazel that seemed more gold than green. Her nose was small and angular and had a light dusting of freckles that crossed its bridge from the center of one eye to the other. Her lips were somewhere between his mother and sister in fullness and a light shade of red, too dark to be called pink. The dress she wore was held up with a single strap on her right shoulder that left the majority of her left side exposed and was a dark blue that contrasted nicely with the golden brown of her hair. Her skin had a faint tan to it, making her seem unpretty by the standards of Rome (who preferred woman to be paler), but Gabriel had always thought the slight glow of sun kissed skin was a much more attractive look. As he looked upon her, he saw that she was wearing a saddened visage.

"Alexandria! What's wrong?" he asked as he relaxed his stiff posture and walked to the waist high wall.

"Gabriel, I'm afraid I have some upsetting news from my father. Are your parents around; I'd really like to tell all of you at once." She really looked saddened by whatever news she was coming to deliver. "May I come in; you and your family shouldn't really be outside for this news."

Walking over to the break in the wall that allowed entry into the yard, Gabriel gestured Alexandria into the yard, ushering her over back to the nook he'd just vacated. "I know what you want to tell me, Alexandria. And I appreciate your sympathies, as well as the fact that you convinced your father not to come here to tell my family this himself." She gave him a confused smile at this, but before she could ask what he meant, he continued, "I know that my sister is dead, with her neck broken and she was found with a lover, near the market on the other side of town. I even know who's responsible."

The look of shock on Alexandria's face as he revealed he already knew all this was quite noticeable. "Gods, I'm sorry Gabriel. She was only discovered an hour ago, I thought that I'd be the one who would have to tell you. But how do you know this, and how do you know who did it?" And there was the keen mind that had first caught his attention.

"Because they're inside my house, dead." A look of fearful apprehension fell across her beautiful features, and Gabriel knew that he had to explain himself further, again. "The witches from the edge of town summoned a demon to kill my family; said demon is the one that killed all those people at the outskirts of town a couple of days ago. After it killed my sister and whoever she was with, it came here to kill the rest of us. After it killed my parents and servant Juba, I was able to subdue it. That brought the witches here to either free the demon or finish what it started. I got very lucky and managed to kill both witches." Seeing the look of revulsion on her face, combined with the shock of it all, Gabriel felt like Alexandria knew what he was feeling right then. "Like I said, I appreciate your sympathies, Alexandria, but I have a few things that I still need to do before I can deal with all this."

"Of-of course, Gabriel," she said. She stood as if to leave, but then sat herself back down. Taking his hand into hers caused Gabriel's eyes to dart from her hand on his to her eyes and back for several seconds. Both blushed as Alexandria seemed to force herself to keep a hold of his hand. "I'll try to ensure that people give you space; but I'm afraid I'll have to tell my father about the death of your parents. I won't tell him what happened, just that your parents are dead too, and that you said you needed time to work it all out." She let go of his hand, but rather than draw away from him, she leaned in closer and wrapped him in a tentative embrace. "If you need anything, anything at all Gabriel, just come to me and I'll help in any way I can," she said softly. Hearing her voice whispered into his ear, sent a shiver of pleasure running down Gabriel's spine.

Feeling brave enough, Gabriel wrapped his arms around her gently and pulled her slightly closer to him. He would've sworn he heard her sigh into his embrace, but that was probably just his wishful thinking and his own exhalation at her being so close. "Thank you, Alexandria," he whispered back, before letting his hands fall back to his side.

"Lexie; my friends call me Lexie," she said as she finally pushed herself away from him and stood. Walking over to the space in the wall, she stopped before she had left the Iracundus property and turned back to him. Her face was sad, but Gabriel could still see the blush on her cheeks. "I am sorry Gabriel. I hope you and your brother can feel better knowing that you were able to bring justice to those who killed your family." Not trusting his voice at the moment, Gabriel just nodded his appreciation to her kindness once again. "I'll, um, I'll let you get back to your grieving." And with that she once again turned to the center of town and left the yard at a pace that seemed faster than she needed to go.

Chapter 22
Medea

Medea had hidden herself upon seeing Gabriel and the stranger in the yard of the Iracundus home, not wanting to impose on the moment they seemed to be sharing. She knew that she had no right to feel it, by any stretch of the imagination, but for the tiniest moment, she felt a twinge of jealousy for whoever this girl was. She was able to offer comfort to the boy, something that Medea would not be able to do as she was still a source of that suffering. Keeping herself out of sight, Medea awaited Gabriel's return inside before she would return to the tragedy at hand. But despite her jealousy, she was glad that Gabriel had someone to offer him comfort.

She didn't have to wait long for him to return. As Gabriel stepped inside, Medea had to hold back the urge to laugh; something about the look on his face seemed to indicate he was pleasantly bemused about whatever had happened outside and the goofy smile that seemed to be stuck on his face for the few seconds before he registered Medea was too precious. Squashing the smile that sneaked out onto her lips, the young witch outstretched her arm pointing deeper into the home. "I've covered the bodies that were in the main room, and laid them down so they aren't posed so disrespectfully. I'll let you get your brother so that we can leave for my home," she said, averting her eyes from the accusation that returned to his once he saw her.

Gabriel simply nodded his understanding, his demeanor taking on a much grimmer disposition as he made his way back to his bedroom. A moment later, he was back, his brother's unconscious body cradled in his arms. Nodding his head toward a hooded robe that hung near the door, he said, "You should put that on; I told my friend whose father is a town elder that the witches at the edge of town were responsible for all this death. I also said that you were dead, so we shouldn't have you parading out in the open. Heaven knows what people would do if they found you alive and in my presence."

It was said with more dispassion than Medea was used to Gabriel speaking with, but she was still thankful that he was concerned for her safety. But then she remembered that she was leading him to her family home so that he could kill her himself, so maybe it wasn't concern but rather a greed to ensure that he alone had the pleasure of ending her life. Deciding it was concern, in a silly attempt to convince herself that Gabriel still cared however minutely about her, Medea took down the robe and threw it over herself, raising the hood to hide her face.

As they walked out into town, Medea could feel the eyes upon them, although she wasn't sure if they were staring at her or Gabriel as he carried his brother. The hooded robe was too conspicuous given her company and the time of day, but she had to respect what little concern Gabriel had for her. Thankfully, the further they went, the less people seemed to stare. And by the time they'd made it out of town their presence was marked with the same indifference as anyone else leaving.

"Can I ask you something?" Gabriel asked out of the blue as they passed the last building that marked the edge of town.

Startled by his making conversation, Medea left the thoughts of her impending death that had consumed her mind for the past twenty minutes. Silently thankful for the distraction from the somber thoughts, Medea nodded. "Of course," she said, a little too eagerly. Coughing to hide the enthusiasm in her reply, she repeated in a slower voice, "Of course, you can. At this point I can't really deny you anything and still feel I have a right to."

"You don't have to answer me out of some sense of duty or propriety. I'll understand if you want to not answer what I'm asking, as it's private." Turning to look at him, Medea gave him a quizzical look. "It has to do with what your mother said," he said as if to elaborate.

Still slightly confused, Medea thought over all her mother had said the night before. Everything seemed to be straight forward, but then she remembered her mother had claimed that she had been in love with Gabriel. Feeling her cheeks flush slightly at the memory, and the look of bewilderment on Gabriel's face as he was told, Medea turned away from his gaze in embarrassment. "You want to know if I'm in love with you," she said. As she still refused to look at him, she had to assume that he nodded to confirm her understanding of his question. But seeing as he didn't contradict her, she assumed that this was indeed what he'd wanted to ask her. "I'm not sure," she said after a moment when she thought that she'd heard him suck in a breath as if he was about to speak. "My mother was right in saying that I betrayed our family for you, that after barely talking to you for an hour I threw my family's legacy away to save you. I barely understand it myself; I was raised to hate you, to believe that your family was the reason that my family was so harassed in this town. And to be honest, that isn't an unfair accusation; something had to be done. But I'd think you'd agree: fighting fire with fire isn't always the best solution."

Forgetting her embarrassment momentarily, Medea turned to look at how Gabriel was taking her answer. But upon seeing his face that seemed to both agree with and be confused by what she said, she quickly turned away again from him. "But that's not related to what you're asking," she corrected in a quiet tone. "Truthfully, I've never really given much thought to love. I always knew that one day I'd have to find a man to father my daughter so that our family coven could continue; but I never really considered my emotions in the equation of who that person would be. But then I was told that I wouldn't get to choose, that Trivia and Terra would guide me to them. And when the vision they gave me showed me only nothing, I broke down. When I finally recovered myself, I returned home. You know what happened next: I lied to my family, convinced them that you were the one who'd father my daughter. Then I ran to you and met you for the first time.

"I'm not going to lie Gabriel, lying to my family about this was a panicked decision that I didn't consider the full consequences of. I hoped that, if by some miracle, my mother and grandmother believed me that they'd call off the demon and rethink their plan. I didn't think that they'd accelerate everything to be over in a night. I didn't think—" Medea stopped herself, thinking how she could convey her rationale. Stopping in her tracks, she turned so her back was to him. "I didn't think…and for that, I'm truly sorry.

"I wasn't opposed to you being the father of my daughter; but I wouldn't want you to suffer the fate that would have awaited you were you to do so. I was barely able to stomach killing my father and all that entailed, I don't think that a daughter born of us would have the stomach to do that for she would be too gentle. Not to mention that she'd want to talk to you, and doing so would make her want to protect you like it did her mother." As she explained the actions of their hypothetical daughter to him, Medea couldn't help but turn back to give a small smile to Gabriel. Finally looking into his eyes, Medea had her answer. "I do love you, Gabriel, but I'm not *in love* with you, if that makes sense. To me you're like the feel of warm sunshine on your skin after a harsh and cold winter; you only realize that you've been craving it after having that experience of a cool and distant sun for half the year."

Gabriel was quiet for a long time as she revealed this. Not wanting him to feel the pressure of this revelation, that he was her only real sense of warmth in life and he was about to kill her, Medea gave him another small smile before turning back toward her home and continuing to walk toward it. She was only a couple of steps ahead of him when she heard the crunch of his feet running to catch up to her. When he'd caught up to her, he said, "Thank you. I know that wasn't easy for you to explain. Although, I'm not sure how I'm supposed to come to terms with literally being your sunshine."

"It's not just for you to come to terms with," Medea replied. "I have to accept that fact as well. But I don't want you to feel burdened by my feelings; they don't really matter at this point."

"Of course, your feelings matter!" Gabriel said automatically; so quickly that Medea had to wonder if this wasn't an instinct.

"Well, if that's the case, indulge my curiosity and tell me who was that girl earlier that sparked a twinge of jealousy in me, the one you were hugging quite tightly."

Medea didn't really expect Gabriel to answer her. If anything, she was almost positive that his response to this question would be either outright dismissal or, the more likely option, he'd tell her that she was his friend just come to offer sympathies and leave it at that. What Medea didn't expect, in any sense, was laughter. But not just a small chuckle; no, Gabriel was doubled over and shaking with gales of laughter that carried across the plain that they walked, almost dropping his brother in the process of trying to keep himself under control.

When after a full minute of laughing he was finally able to calm himself, Gabriel's smile was short lived as he turned back toward town. When he turned back to her, Medea noticed that what had been a happy smile was now a sad one tugging his lips up into the faintest traces of a smile. "Thank you, I really needed a good laugh."

The sad smile on his face brightened the slightest bit, but Medea wanted to make the happy one return. "Then why are you so sad about having laughed in the first place?" she asked while tentatively placing a consoling hand on his arm and rubbing gently when he didn't flinch away.

They'd stopped walking again as he took a deep, noisy breath. Awaiting his answer, Medea simply continued to rub his arm, shifting from his arm to his back after a few moments of him not saying anything. "For the same reason I laughed in the first place: my sister, Mary."

"Oh, I didn't mean—"

"No, it's alright. The girl you saw me with early is named Alexandria. I'm laughing at the fact that you got jealous over the hug, because it reminded me of the other night when Mary got jealous of you kissing my cheek. My sister and I haven't been close for a decade, despite our being twins. But the past couple of days we've been—" Medea felt him tense as he cut himself off, but his starting to walk again didn't register to Medea as an attempt to remove himself from her touch. So, while she stopped rubbing, she kept her hand on his back to show that she was still there and supportive of him. "The past couple of days me and Mary were regaining that closeness we once shared. But the night that we met, my sister told me that she, correctly, suspected you to be one of the witches that cursed us, but that she thought you were interested in the two of us being intimate." A bashful smile creeped out onto his face, making the flush of embarrassment stand out even more.

"Mary wanted me to try and seduce you into revealing yourself as the witch, and how to lift the curse you and your family had placed upon us. She said that with her knowledge in the art of seduction, my good looks, and your clear interest, that you'd be telling us everything within a week. I didn't want to use her plan, but as we didn't have any attack plan for dealing with all this, I agreed to it. Knowing that I was uncomfortable, to say the least, Mary promised me something that I have longed for in return.

"Over the years, my sister has apparently been searching this town to find me a wife. And the only person that met her standards was Alexandria; which worked out for me because I've been interested in her for a while. And having you feel jealous of her is just funny because this all started with my sister being jealous of both you and her. Or should I say of me."

Medea gave him a confused look at his correction which caused him to look away in what she thought was shame. "Mary was, ah, shall we say a very open and loving person. And in all her life there was only one person who refused her affections repeatedly: Alexandria. She was greatly annoyed by this, but she knew there had to be a reason, and she figured that reason was me. She learned that Alexandria was saving herself for her husband, and it would seem that both Mary and Alexandria think that could and should be me." Blushing, he turned from her gaze.

"Well, allow me to offer my support and encouragement of this union. And if so many different women agree on something, it's usually a good sign to take it." The smile Medea gave him was a gentle tease. "But I wasn't jealous of this Alexandria because I thought you loved her; I was jealous because she was giving you comfort, when I cannot." Her smile now faded, Medea finally removed her hand from Gabriel's back and forced herself a step ahead of him.

"Oh," was all Gabriel said to this. "I-I uh, I appreciate the attempt."

Despite herself, Medea gave a light chuckle at this. “You don’t need to be so polite with me, Gabriel; please feel free to hate me as you need. I will not hold your wrath against you, I welcome it even. Like you, I appreciate the attempt, but please do not feel obligated to be so kind to me; lest we forget, I’m leading you to my home so that you may kill me and burn my ancestral home to the ground. I know you are kind, but neither your god nor mine would hold it against you for feeling anger toward someone so integrally responsible for the death of your family. In fact, killing me isn’t a sin, as not only am I telling you to do so, in doing so, you’re also protecting what little family you have left,” Medea said with a nod toward the boy in his arms.

Stopping beside the tree that was her home, she lovingly placed a hand on the trunk. “We’re here,” she said, not allowing him to respond to her outburst about him hating her. “Wait here while I grab the sickle inside.” Turning her back to him, she walked through the trunk and into her home.

Chapter 23
Gabriel

As he waited for her return, Gabriel tried to sort out all his emotions that had been weighing him down since he'd been awoken by Medea late last night. Chief among them was grief, at having lost his family in such a way. But there was also anger at Medea and her family for having caused all this, guilt at not being there for his sister one last time, and worry for how his brother would deal with all this and the trauma of having physically been the one to kill everyone. So much pain and anguish swirled around in his head. He thought that he'd burst apart into a thousand pieces with everything that he felt.

But there was more, deeper down.

All his surface level emotions were understandable, but in the back of his mind and the bottom of his heart, Gabriel knew that these emotions weren't really what was causing the turmoil he felt. What caused these emotions were feelings that he didn't know exactly why he felt them, but he still did. Guilt and shame for having to kill Medea and her family, anger at his family for being so hostile to those that didn't follow God while not always following Him themselves, hatred for his brother for having killed their family. There was the disgust at his sister at what she'd asked him to do.

Gabriel knew these feeling contradicted each other. But he couldn't deny that these were all vying to be what he felt the most, to be what he would act upon. To keep himself together though, Gabriel forced himself to cling tightly to only two of the emotions that raged like the storm last night inside him: his sadness at the loss of his family and the glimmer of hope for a future as Alexandria's husband. Why he was clinging to that emotion, he couldn't fully say. Perhaps it was because it was something he'd harbored long before all this had started; or maybe it was because he needed to feel something positive and happy amongst all the negative and destructive emotions that were aswirl inside the all too small confines that were his head and heart.

Kneeling himself down, Gabriel gently laid Marcus II down on the ground at his side. Staying on his knees, Gabriel straightened himself up. With his right hand, he crossed himself as he began to pray. "Forgive me, Lord God, for I have and am about to sin," he quietly said, his head bowed in both shame and reverence. "I killed the two witches who had cursed my family, and will kill the third in the next few moments. It was not my wish to do these things, but in order to protect what family I have left, it has become my responsibility. I pray You see these actions, not as the unforgivable acts that they are, but sinful acts taken for the greater good and survival of my family. I've always tried to live in such a way that my words and actions were inoffensive to all and to treat everyone with respect. Please, in Your wisdom and mercy, judge me forgivable."

Raising his head, Gabriel looked back toward town. "Forgive my family, Almighty God. I don't know all their sins, nor do I believe all of them to be justified in being committed, but since they were taken from this world before they were able to properly atone for their sins themselves, I ask You judge them leniently, or give them a chance to redeem themselves. When I die, should I be worthy of entering Heaven, I wish to see them again. I miss them so much already, and know that this yearning for them will only grow as time goes on."

Hearing footsteps to his side, Gabriel swung his head to find Medea standing before the tree she had disappeared into minutes earlier. As their eyes met, he saw a smile pull the corners of her mouth up, as she turned herself around to give him the privacy she clearly thought he wanted. In a voice slightly louder than the one he had been using, just loud enough that he knew that she could hear what he said, Gabriel continued, "Forgive the women whose blood will forever stain my hands, Lord. They may have scorned Your faith and tried to have it erased from the land, committing numerous sins to do so, but their actions weren't always unjustified. You gave us the gift of free will so that we may live our lives how we chose, even if that life was sinful in Your eyes. These women were not devout in faith of You, but the faith they practiced had their entire devotion, and had people like my family not persecuted them, they may have yet lived good lives."

As he asked God to forgive Medea and her family, he'd watched the girl to see what her reaction would be. All she did was bow her head and bring her hand to her heart. "Forgive us God Almighty. Our Father, who art in Heaven, hallowed be Thy name. Thy kingdom come, Thy will be done, on Earth as it is in Heaven. Give us this day our daily bread and forgive us our trespasses, as we forgive those who trespass against us. And lead us not into temptation, but deliver us from evil. Amen." Signing himself with the cross once again, Gabriel stood up.

Walking over to her, he placed his hand on Medea's shoulder and gently turned her to face him. Seeing the faint tracks her tears had caused to form on her face, he gently wiped her cheeks and eyes to stop her tears. But he thought it was the shock of having him wipe away her tears that truly made her stop crying. When he'd finally stopped wiping and had returned his hands to his side, Medea looked at him with awed confusion. "Why? Why do you constantly do things that make me love you? We should hate each other; we are responsible for the deaths of the other's family. You made me betray my family with a single conversation; I placed protection on you, and you alone, rather than on your entire family. We have every reason to hate each other, and yet, you insist upon words and actions that make my heart scream in longing. Sweet Terra, why do you inflict this blissful torture upon me?"

There was no anger in her voice; truthfully her voice seemed to be devoid of all emotion except exasperation. Before he could respond to her, Gabriel felt the air leave his lungs as Medea threw her arms around his torso in a crushing hug. "Thank you, Gabriel," she whispered into his chest. "Thank you for doing the hardest thing in your religion: thank you for asking your god to forgive my family, despite all that we did against you. I know that doing so could not have been easy; and even if your plea was disingenuous, the fact that you asked shows that you are a better person than I could hope to be."

No sooner had he placed his hand upon her back, returning her hug, that she pushed herself away from him. Her awkward contrite smile on her lips, and her eyes avoiding his, Gabriel quietly but firmly said, "You're welcome." Her face turned to look upon him intently at hearing his words.

A blush creeped across the girl's pale skin. Clearly trying to alleviate the embarrassment she felt, Medea stiffly thrust out her right hand that held the lead sickle. "Umm, you need this," she said opening her hand palm up so he could take it. But the imbalance of the blade and handle caused the sickle to fall to the ground. Both of them bent down to pick it up at the same time, causing them to smack their heads against together in their haste to grab it. "Sorry, sorry," Medea espoused as she retrieved the sickle with one hand and rubbed her head with the other. Straightening up, she forcefully but gently pushed the sickle flat against Gabriel's chest, not letting go until his hand left rubbing the sore spot on his head to grab it. "Sorry," she whispered again.

Embarrassed himself at the encounter, Gabriel turned himself slightly away from her. "Me too," he whispered. Looking anywhere but at her, he found his eyes resting upon his brother. Glancing down to the lead sickle in his hand, Gabriel swallowed the lump that had suddenly risen in his throat as he turned back to Medea, his face a mask that hid the turmoil within him. "Where do you want to do this?" he asked.

Upon hearing and seeing the seriousness of his demeanor, Medea seemed to force the residual embarrassment she still felt down, as she looked first to him and then around what he assumed was her home. "Bring your brother here," she said solemnly. "Ideally, I'd wait for the new moon in two days' time; I was born under a full moon, seems only fitting that I'd die under a new one. But since it must be now, right here will have to do," she said as Gabriel went to retrieve his brother. Lying herself onto the ground, she placed her hands under her breasts just below her sternum. "Place him beside me so that when my last breath leaves me and the spell giving you protection fades, causing the demon to wake, you can act quickly to decapitate the snake that houses it. The more time you waste in killing it, the more strength it will regain and the more likely it will escape. Your brother should wake within a minute or two after the demon has left his body."

As Gabriel finished placing Marcus to be in the same pose as Medea had assumed, he turned himself back to her. Once again on his knees, he brought the sickle up to her throat. But for all his might and concentration, he couldn't make the blade stay steady, his hand shook too much. Finally giving up after a minute, Gabriel dropped his arm to his side. "I-I-I can't do it. I can't kill you Medea!" he said.

Propping herself up on her elbows, Medea gave him a look of such empathy that Gabriel felt a tear or two start to well up in his eyes. Here was this girl, who by all accounts he should hate, willingly sacrificing herself for his safety, all but begging him to kill her, and in her eyes was an understanding so complete that he almost couldn't fathom what had led her to feeling it. Sitting herself up so that their eyes were level, Medea placed her hand over his and gave it a gentle squeeze. "Yes, yes you can, Gabriel. You must. You have already confessed to killing me to your god; you don't want to have you're not doing this make you a liar and thus tarnishing your pleas for forgiveness. I know that you can do this, Gabriel. It may be painful and the guilt may consume you; but don't look at this as killing that which you hate, look at it as protecting something you love," she said with a nod to his brother on Gabriel's other side. "My death is divine justice for the many wrongs that both me and my family have committed not only against your family, but the innocents of this town. You can enact the will of both our gods Gabriel, grim as it is."

Lying herself back down, Medea brought his hand holding the lead sickle back up to her throat. But when she let go of his hand, it shook even more erratically than before. Tears began to flow down his cheeks as he put all his effort in trying to make his hand stay steady. When after a minute it was still shaking, he dropped his arm to his side and let go of the handle as if it was searing hot, causing a dull clang to sound as the blade rattled on the ground. "I know I should hate you, Medea, but I don't. How can I hate someone who has sacrificed so much for me, someone who has loved me for as long as she's known me and helped me with all her might." His eyes sought out hers as he was about to reveal something that was becoming more and more clear to him the more time he spent with her. "I love you too, Medea."

The stillness of the air around them was all that allowed Gabriel to hear the small gasp that she let out upon hearing this. His eyes were focused solely on hers, watching as they widened as his words registered in her head. It was only when she closed her eyes that Gabriel took stock of the rest of her. Her hands had risen to her chest, over her heart, as a serene, if saddened, smile ghosted her lips. Again sitting up, Medea wrapped her arms around his neck as she pulled him into another hug. But unlike her last hug, this one was gentle and Gabriel could almost feel the love and gratitude that she seemed to want the hug to represent. "Thank you, Gabriel, feeling the love of another is such a rare occurrence in my life, it will be nice to die having felt it one last time."

Not knowing how or what to respond to this, Gabriel wrapped his arms around her as gently as she held him. It was a few moments before either of them let the other go. Gabriel could only speak for himself, but he assumed that this hug was about more than their love for the other; it was about their sorrow at having to part, their guilt for causing the other pain, the emptiness their recent losses at the hands of the other had left in them and all the other contradictory and confused emotions that they felt for each other. When she finally did let him go, the two of them took a moment to wipe away the tears that had silently fell as they held the other.

Rather than lying down again, as he thought she would, Medea interlaced her fingers in his. "Do you know the tale of Achilles and Penthesilea?" she asked.

Confused by her sudden change of subject, especially to something so random, Gabriel gave her a quizzical look but answered her question anyways. "Not particularly well. Wasn't she an Amazonian queen that he killed during the Trojan War shortly after killing Hector?"

Nodding, Medea continued, "Yes, but there's more to their tale, at least in the version that my mother told me when I was younger. After having dragged Hector's body around the city for a third time, Achilles pauses to verbally taunt the Trojans, claiming that Hector was no challenge and the city was doomed to ruin if that was their best fighter. My mother also claimed that he yelled to them that their mothers smelled of elderberries and that their fathers were hamsters, but I think that was more to make me laugh than something that he really said." The both of them gave small chuckles to this.

"As a daughter of Mars, Penthesilea took great offense to Achilles' mocking and the flaunting of his disregard for the rules of war. Taking a handful of the warriors she'd brought to Troy, she strode out of the city to face Achilles. But upon seeing the advancement of her forces, a battalion of Greek soldiers rushed to encircle Achilles. It should have been a quick slaughter of a fight, 200 men against ten women. But as time passed, two things became clear: the Amazons were better fighters than the Greeks and only Achilles stood a chance against them.

"While the Amazons defeated all the Greeks that had come to Achilles' defense, it took Achilles fighting with three other men to take down each Amazon, until only the queen and hero were left. Despite his wrath being in full force at this point, Achilles concedes that the Amazons are great warriors and bemoans his being their opponent, that he wishes to not see the fall of the great warrior culture. Penthesilea rages at the implication that her culture will fall, and that Achilles himself will be their downfall. In her indignation she attacks him, denting his armor made by

Vulcan himself and is even able to draw blood despite the protection of the River Styx.

"But despite all this, Achilles kills her. But as he runs her through with his sword, the two of them end up in a lover's embrace, their lips coming together in a brief but lustful passion and Achilles inhales her last breath. He lays her gently on the ground, requesting Pluto be kind with her soul.

"As he returns the Greek camp, a soldier named Thersites claims that Achilles just showed Penthesilea more tenderness than he'd ever shown Patroclus and thus implying that Achilles loved the Amazonian queen more than he did Patroclus. Achilles stops in his tracks, walks back to Thersites and stabs the hilt of his sword through his face." Her version of the tale over, Medea gave a brief pause before she continued. "Personally, I believe that Achilles did fall in love with Penthesilea in those moments on the battlefield. It wasn't enough to come anywhere near eclipsing his love for Patroclus, but there's a type of love that isn't nearly discussed enough that only enemies can feel for each other."

Upon hearing her words, Gabriel knew why she'd brought up this story. Squeezing her hand that was interlaced with his gently, he nodded as he didn't trust himself to speak at that moment. With the delicateness of plucking a flower, Gabriel brought her hand to his lips before planting a gentle kiss on each of her fingertips. Letting go of her hand, he softly returned it to her breast, her heart, as he put pressure on it to have her lie back down. But her slight resistance at his pressure caused him to search out her eyes and the answer he hoped to find within.

"Can I ask you for one last favor, Gabriel?" Her voice was meek but she held his gaze. "One last thing that you do before I die?"

Eager to prolong his taking her life for as long as possible, Gabriel nodded his head vigorously. "Yes, anything, Medea."

Smiling at his enthusiasm, Medea asked, "Will you kiss me?"

Slightly taken aback by the request, although he shouldn't have been, given the story she'd just told, Gabriel brought both hands up to her face. Gently cupping her cheeks, he pulled her into himself. Having never kissed a girl before, Gabriel knew the kiss couldn't have been everything that Medea had hoped it would be, but hoped that she felt the same wondrous sensations that he felt as her lips danced with his.

He was surprised when she pulled herself away, before returning to her original position on the ground. Gripping the lead sickle in his hand, Gabriel brought the blade to her throat, the tremors that had caused his hand to shake uncontrollably were now gone. Looking to her eyes one last time, he tried to return the ocean that he saw she felt in that moment. With a quick swing of his elbow, before his courage could flee once again, he cut her throat.

Where Gabriel thought Medea would start to sputter and choke on her own blood as fear flooded her eyes, he was surprised by her actual reaction. Her eyes widened slightly as the cut was made, but that was all. She didn't panic, didn't choke on her blood; she stoically kept her eyes on him, the love and guilt she had felt the entire day still in her eyes.

When her eyes finally glazed over, Gabriel turned back to look at his brother. Unsettled by the black viscous smoke that oozed slowly from his neck, Gabriel gripped and regripped the sickle in his hand as he awaited the demon snake to emerge from his brother's body. Over the course of the next couple of minutes, the smoke that oozed from his brother slowly solidified into the body of cat snake. As it slithered away in a manner that reminded Gabriel of someone either drunk or severely wounded, he raised the sickle over his head. Once the snake was clear of his brother's body, Gabriel swung with all the force he could muster, taking the snake's head off an inch from the base of its skull.

Both the head and the body of the snake turned to ash, before melting into the ground. Dropping the sickle, Gabriel cradled his brother in his arms, silently praying that he would wake. Not a minute later, Marcus began to stir in his arms and Gabriel gave both a sigh of relief and a shout of delight. Once his brother's eyes opened, Gabriel pulled the boy into the tightest hug he'd ever given. It was only when he felt Marcus II pushing him away that Gabriel allowed the boy to escape his embrace, but he kept his hands on his brother's shoulders. "Are you alright, Marcus?"

"I think so," the boy said as he looked around. "Where are we Gabriel? And where is everyone?"

Shaking his head as tears once again stung at his eyes, Gabriel pulled his brother into another tight hug. "That doesn't matter right now," he said into the boy's ear. "All that matters is that you are alive and well and that the curse on our family is broken."

Picking his brother up as he stood, Gabriel tried to ensure that Marcus didn't see Medea's body on the ground behind him. Walking away back to town, Gabriel stopped two trees away from the one that Medea had indicated as her home. Shifting his brother to his other arm, he pulled his knife from his hip. Quickly gouging out two slashes into the trunk of the tree so he knew where to go, Gabriel returned his knife to its sheath and continued on.

*

Knocking on the door, Gabriel held his despondent brother close to his side. As they had returned to town, Gabriel had informed his brother that their family was dead, causing the young boy to cry for an hour non-stop. Gabriel had cried too, finally allowing all his grief to be felt. They'd stayed outside of town for the next thirty minutes as they composed themselves. But rather than returning to their home, Gabriel had taken them to a different destination: the home of Elder Antonius.

Looking out to the setting sun, Gabriel awaited the opening of the door. As it was the time of day when many families ate supper, he figured that he might need to knock again to draw attention to his presence. He was about to raise his hand to knock again when the door opened to reveal a girl no more than fifteen in a dirty white dress. With her head bowed as she asked who they were and what business they had with Elder Antonius, Gabriel knew the girl was a servant. "I wish to speak with Elder Antonius and his daughter Alexandria. My name is Gabriel Iracundus."

The girl's head snapped up to look upon him as he said his name. She opened the door wider and ushered them inside. "Please wait here, Master Iracundus. I will inform my mistress and her father that you are here." He didn't know what it was, but Gabriel thought that the girl's voice had changed as she welcomed them into the home, as if it had gotten bolder.

"Father hates Elder Antonius, Gabriel; why are we here?" his brother asked in confusion once the servant girl had left to retrieve Alexandria and her father. "I want to go home."

"I know you want to go home, Marcus; I do too. But home isn't fit to have us be there right now. When she came to tell me about Mary this morning, Alexandria offered me all that she could give to help us as much as possible. And we're here to greatly accept some of that assistance."

Before Marcus could complain and argue some more, the sound of footsteps alerted them to the approach of Alexandria and Elder Antonius. Looking to the hallway that led from the entryway, Gabriel saw the two being led to them by the serving girl who'd let them in. As he gazed upon Alexandria, Gabriel couldn't help the smile that sprang forth. Something that he saw was mirrored on the young woman's face, as well as blushing of her cheeks.

Bowing himself at the waist for a moment, once the Elder and his daughter had entered the entryway, Gabriel began his request. "Pardon the interruption and intrusion, Elder Antonius, but my brother and I are in need of your assistance."

"It must be something great if you're here at this time of night, interrupting my family's dinner," the old man said, a not-so-subtle scowl upon his face.

"Father!" Alexandria said indignantly. "They've just lost their family, show some compassion." As she turned to look back at Gabriel, Alexandria's face softened. "What is it you need, Gabriel? As I told you this morning, I'll help in any way I can."

Smiling his gratitude to her, Gabriel forced himself to look back upon her father. "I'm here to ask you for a place to stay. The attack on my home has left it a mess that I do not wish my brother to see. If it's not too much trouble, would it be alright if we stayed here for a few days until I remove the things that would traumatize my brother further?"

"Of cour—" Alexandria started to say, before her father raised his hand and commanded her silence.

"Before I agree to this, if I agree to this, master Iracundus, answer me this: why here? It is no secret that your father and I were hostile to one another, nor is it a secret that my family and I still practice the faith that your father called pagan devil worship. So I want to know why you've come to me seeking shelter when there are others of your own faith, people your family surely held in higher esteem than me and mine, that would help you more eagerly than I would." The wrinkles on his face nearly doubled as he glared at him.

"I hadn't really given much thought to it, to be honest. As Alexandria said, she offered any assistance that she could give this morning. I was simply looking to take a friend up on their offer to help." Gabriel hoped that his telling of the truth would be enough to convince Elder Antonius. "But if you would rather we go somewhere else, just say the word and we'll be on our way."

It was a tense moment as the old man deliberated his decision. "As my daughter said, master Iracundus, you may stay. But only for a week, after that, you will not be welcome."

Bowing again, Gabriel said, "Thank you, Elder Antonius; I'll try to make our stay as smooth as possible."

"See that you do," he said before he turned to his daughter. "Since this is all your doing, I'll leave it to you to find them suitable lodging and to see that their needs are met."

"Yes, Father," Alexandria responded. Waiting for her father to return to what Gabriel assumed was the dining room, Gabriel saw Alexandria turn to the girl at her side, which seemed to be her personal servant. "Julia, will you take the young master Iracundus to the bedroom beside mine." The girl nodded to her mistress' command, as Alexandria crouched down to his brother's eye level. "It's Marcus, right?" she asked, to which his brother nodded. "Are you hungry Marcus? Just tell me what you'd like to eat and I'll have Anthony prepare it for you."

"Roasted chicken and potatoes, please Lady Alexandria," Marcus said after Gabriel gave him a reassuring nod.

"Roasted chicken and potatoes it is then," Alexandria said. Straightening up, she turned back to Julia, "After you settle him into the room, inform Anthony of his choice in meal."

"Yes Mistress," the girl said. Offering her hand to his brother, Gabriel watched silently as the girl led Marcus deeper into the home.

"Do you want to sleep in the same room as your brother, or do you want to sleep somewhere else?" Alexandria asked once they were alone; startling him with how close she seemed to have gotten to him without his noticing.

"I think it best if we stay together," he answered. Looking into her hazel eyes, Gabriel felt himself begin to fall into the golden green pools that held the intelligence that had always captured his attention. Realizing that he'd been staring, Gabriel forced his eyes away from hers, unintentionally having them land on her breasts. Flushing crimson, he turned away from her until she was just at the edge of his vision. "Thank you, Al-Lexie," he said, remembering to use her nickname. "Your father wouldn't have let us stay if you hadn't convinced him. And I appreciate that very much."

Placing her hand on his shoulder, causing him to once again look at her, Alexandria smiled at him. "Of course, Gabriel; what are friends for if not helping you in your times of need. I'm just glad that you took my offer, rather than try to be stoically masculine and dealing with all this alone."

"Well, that makes me more comfortable in asking you for another favor," he said with a gentle smile. "Well, two actually."

Sliding her hand from his shoulder, down his arm and into his hand, she smiled at him as she gently tugged him into her home. "Name it, Gabriel; I already told you that I'll help in any way I can. But you probably haven't eaten all day, so come to the dining room and have the rest of my dinner."

Planting his feet so that she was no longer leading him, Gabriel gave a gentle tug on the hand that was still miraculously in his. "I don't want to have anything in my stomach that I could lose later," he said, causing Alexandria to give him a look of confusion. "There's something that I still need to do before I can sleep tonight, and I'm not sure how I'll react while doing it." Upon hearing his vague answer to her unspoken question, her eyes looked deep into his, blazing bright as they searched for answers. "Which brings me back to my requests."

"What do you need Gabriel?"

"A horse and cart, and for you to watch my brother until I return."

Alexandria simply studied him for a moment before answering him. "It's very kind of you, Gabriel; and probably more than those women deserve, especially from you."

"What do you mean?"

"You're going to bury the witches that killed your family," she said simply. When she saw his look of confusion as to how she'd determined this, she elaborated, "You want a horse and cart, implying that you can't or won't carry whatever it is you need. You're wanting to leave now, rather than waiting for morning, which means you want to do this at night and thus eliminate the possibility that you'll be seen, ergo you don't want to be seen doing this. Your refusal to eat because whatever you're doing has the potential to cause you to throw it up, meaning that you are slightly disgusted by doing this, but feel you must. Add all that up, plus your general compassion and belief in the golden rule, as well as your need to have your home made livable again, it really can only be concluded that you're going to bury the witches that killed your parents and sister. A generous act, that I commend you on, but I personally think that it's something that is beyond what those women deserve. Especially from one of their intended victims."

Stunned slightly by her deductions, and the speed she was able to correctly reach them, Gabriel had to hold himself back from kissing her. It was hardly the time, and he still wasn't sure how she felt about him, despite his sister's insistence that she harbored feeling for him. "Like you said, it's something that I feel that I have to do, deserved or not; I'm probably the only one who would do it. Will you help me like I've asked?"

Nodding, Alexandria started to once again pull him deeper into her home. "You should say goodnight to your brother, as well as familiarize yourself with where you'll be staying for the next week."

*

An hour after the last light of day had faded, and the light of the moon shone bright and clear, Gabriel found himself once again outside the tree that had been the house for Medea and her family. Three mounds of earth, two of which were unmarked and the third having a rudimentary cross, marked the graves of the coven of witches. Breathing heavy from the exertion of having dug and then filled the graves, Gabriel leaned on the shovel he'd used as he struggled to find the words. "I, uh…I don't know what to say, Medea. I barely know the practices that my religion uses when laying our dead to rest; let alone a culture I barely knew existed until a couple of days ago." Running his hands through his hair, before bringing them back to his face and scrubbing as if he were washing clothes in the river. "Please do not be offended by my lack of knowledge, I've left you each a solidus for Charon's toll; I hope it's enough." Still not knowing what to say, Gabriel began to pace the graves slightly.

Stopping after a minute of pacing once again at the foot of Medea's grave. "I'm sorry that you had to die for this all to be over, Medea. It's not fair that I get to live on and spread my faith further out into the world, while you are dead and your faith will most likely be demonized by those that come after. I can't control the actions of others, but I promise that I'll preach tolerance and acceptance for all, regardless of creed. Christ didn't condemn those that didn't follow Him, He simply wished them to live just lives that benefited everyone." Pausing as he wondered if he should bring up Christ at a moment like this, Gabriel looked around in search of answers to questions he couldn't form. "Goodbye Medea; I hope that you find peace in death, and that whatever gods you worshipped welcome you into their company."

Picking up the torch that'd lit his way, Gabriel leaned it against the tree that had been the witches' home. Within minutes, it was ablaze; flames danced along its trunk and branches in a rainbow of colors. Whatever magic had once been housed there, was going up in flames with the rest of the family home. It was beautiful to watch as the night grew brighter and warmer from the inferno. Once the larger branches began to snap and fall to the ground, Gabriel walked back to the horse and cart that Alexandria had given him to use. Sliding into the saddle, he urged the horse away from the burning tree that miraculously wasn't spreading its blaze to the trees around it.

With a final glance up to the sliver moon, Gabriel noted that it was the first time in a while since he'd seen the moon unobstructed by clouds, as he had Alexandria's horse return them to town.

CPSIA information can be obtained
at www.ICGtesting.com
Printed in the USA
LVHW051319230623
750602LV00005B/69

9 781685 629441